'... keeps you ...

... book down! I'd give this book 10 out of 10
... ause it is adventurous and exciting.' *Harriet,*
... Evening Echo

... six rumbustious adventures, it enjoys
... ...onesque jollities and gorgeous grotesques
drawn by Ted Dewan.' *Amanda Craig, The Times*

THOMAS TREW
AND THE SELKIE'S CURSE

SOPHIE MASSON

Illustrated by Ted Dewan

Hodder
Children's
Books

A division of Hachette Children's Books

With thanks to
Year 4 of Gomer Junior School, Gosport, Hampshire

Copyright © 2007 Sophie Masson
Illustrations copyright © 2007 Ted Dewan

First published in Great Britain in 2007
by Hodder Children's Books

A Catalogue record for this book is available from
the British Library

ISBN-13: 978 0 340 89487 3

Typeset in Weiss by Avon DataSet Ltd,
Bidford on Avon, Warwickshire

Printed and bound in Great Britain by
Clays Ltd, St Ives plc

The paper and board used in this paperback by Hodder Children's
Books are natural recyclable products made from wood grown in
sustainable forests. The manufacturing processes conform to the
environmental regulations of the country of origin.

Hodder Children's Books
a division of Hachette Children's Books
338 Euston Road, London NW1 3BH
An Hachette Livre UK Company

For Nell and Will Shepherd

Dear Reader,

Do you wish you could leave the ordinary world and go into an extraordinary world, one full of fun and magic and adventure – and danger? You do? Well, so does Thomas Trew – and one grey London afternoon, his wish comes true!

Two amazing people come calling at his house – a dwarf called Adverse Camber and a bright little lady named Angelica Eyebright. They tell Thomas he's a Rymer and that he has a destiny in their world, the world of the Hidden People. And they ask him to come and live in their village, Owlchurch, which lies deep in the Hidden World.

It's a world of magic – what the Hidden People call 'pishogue'. It's a world of extraordinary places and people – the Ariels, who live in the sky; the Seafolk, who live in the ocean; the Montaynards, who live in the rocks and mountains; the Uncouthers, who live deep underground, and the Middlers, who live on the surface of the earth. Not everyone in the Hidden World is pleasant or friendly, and some of them, like the Uncouthers, are very nasty indeed . . .

All kinds of adventures are waiting for Thomas in the Hidden World. And this is just one of them. Look out for the others, too!

ONE

Pinch Gull hurried along the river path. It was very late. Moonlight fell in pale stripes on the path and turned the river to shining silver. It was very quiet. Too quiet. There was no owl-call, no rustle of night-animals, not even the sound of water lapping at the bank.

Pinch was beginning to wish he was safely at home in bed. But it would very soon be midnight. And at exactly midnight, a silver finger of moonlight would reach into the deep black shadow under the twisted old willow tree and touch the blue moon-clover plant growing under it. Its tiny flowers would open at once. Picked then, the clover had a rare power, infusing ointments and potions with a double dose of night-magic.

It was going to be a surprise for his mother, Old Gal. Nobody else had seen the plant, and he hadn't told anyone about it. He had only seen it by accident that morning, playing handball with his twin sister Patch and his human friend Thomas Trew. Looking for the ball in the long grass near the willow, his eye caught a flash of pale blue. He peered closer. Wow! Blue moon-clover! Moon-clover was usually white, and fairly common. But blue moon-clover was very rare.

It had all seemed fun and exciting when he'd sneaked out of the sleeping cottage. But now he wished he'd told Patch and Thomas. The night didn't feel friendly. It felt as though eyes were watching him. Perhaps it was just the trees. Occasionally they pulled themselves up and walked around. They didn't like being spied on by people, though. The willows were especially crabby sorts. And that twisted old willow was likely to be the most crabby of the lot. 'Well,' Pinch told himself, 'even if it happens, they know my dad's the Green Man, and that ought to make them more friendly.'

He'd almost reached the willow – to his relief it seemed to be standing perfectly still, in its usual place – when he smelled a smell. A stink, in fact, of stagnant water and rotting waterweed. Ugh! Smells like Peg Powler, he thought. But what was she doing here?

Peg Powler was a dangerous solitary who lived in a deep dark waterhole by the forest. She was useful, because she prevented Uncouthers from coming up through the waterhole. But nobody liked her. She had long green teeth and was always hungry. You wouldn't want to stumble into her waterhole by mistake. But she wasn't allowed to hunt here.

Just then, Pinch heard a familiar drawl.

'Is this all on the level, Peg?'

That was the Lady Pandora speaking! Along with Mr Tamblin, she was one of the

Mayors of Aspire, the glamorous village across the river. Interesting – why was the supercool Lady Pandora hobnobbing with stinky old Peg Powler?

'Of course it is, my lady,' said Peg Powler, in an injured voice. 'As if Nelly and I would lie to you!'

Pinch raised his eyebrows. Nelly Long Arms was Peg Powler's cousin, and about as nice as Peg herself. She lived at the river-mouth.

Pandora snorted. 'What do you think, Calliope?'

Calliope! So the Owlchurch music-maker was mixed up in this midnight meeting too! What *was* going on? Burning with curiosity, and forgetting all about the clover, Pinch climbed quietly up the tree. He peered through the leaves.

The moonlight was very bright, and he could see quite a way down the bank. And there they were! Peg Powler crouched in the scummy foam at the edge of the water, looking

4

up at Lady Pandora, tall and slim in a cream and navy suit, and round little Calliope Nightingale, shawls wrapped around her, a rather silly three-cornered hat on her springy hair. Heart beating fast, Pinch leaned forward to listen better.

'I think we must take it seriously,' said Calliope. She turned to Peg Powler. 'Why did they send Nelly, though, and not one of their own messengers?'

'Too risky,' said Peg, promptly. She tapped the side of her nose. 'All very hush-hush. Ears and eyes everywhere, see? 'Sides, we're sort of distant relations, see? Water-blood will tell, oh yes it will, even if sweetwater we, saltwater they.'

They must be talking about the Seafolk, thought Pinch. But which ones? There were lots of different tribes of Seafolk.

'Hmph,' said Calliope. 'I'm surprised, still, that they used you and Nelly as messengers.'

Peg shrugged. 'That's the way it is. Well, you

comin' or not, ladies? They specially said not to tarry.'

Calliope said, slowly, 'I'd like to consult Angelica Eyebright. The Mayor of Owlchurch needs to know what's going on.'

'No time to waste, they said. Come now or it'll be too late. You don't want that on your conscience, do you, ladies?' Peg's green smile flashed. Pinch shuddered.

'It's no good, Calliope,' said Pandora, firmly. 'We've got to get to the bottom of this. Angelica and Tamblin would both agree. It might not be as bad as we fear, but inaction could be very dangerous. I'm ready if you are. What do you say?'

Calliope sighed. 'Very well.' She waded into the river, took off her hat and laid it on the water. She took out a silver flute and played a trill of notes on it. At once, the hat turned into a graceful swan-shaped boat. Calliope hopped on, as did the Lady Pandora. In the water, Peg Powler circled them, her

6

movements smooth and constant, like a shark's.

Then a breeze sprang up – a magic breeze, for it only blew behind the boat – and the little craft began to glide down the river, faster and faster. Soon, it was lost to sight around a bend of the river, and shortly after Peg Powler also swam out of sight.

Pinch waited a moment before clambering down. It was only then that he remembered the blue moon-clover. He hurried around to the other side of the tree. Too late! The moonlight had already been and gone on the little plant. Its flowers hung drooping, and it was beginning to wither. Blast! thought Pinch. He picked the plant anyway and shoved it in his pocket. Then he took off up the path, as fast as he could possibly go.

TWO

Pinch headed into the village, to the Apple Tree Café, where his friend Thomas lived. He hoped Thomas might still be awake, reading.

Yes! There was a light on upstairs, in Thomas's bedroom window. Pinch picked up some pebbles and threw them at the glass. Thomas appeared. Pinch beckoned him down.

Out in the street, Thomas looked half-asleep. 'What's up?' he yawned.

'Weird stuff,' said Pinch, and began to explain, his words tumbling over each other.

When he'd finished, Thomas said, 'But can't you guess what they were talking about?'

Pinch shook his head. 'Something bad

happening in Seafolk country. I don't have a clue exactly what.'

'But obviously to do with Middlers too.'

'Yeah. But it's odd. Peg said the people who gave the message were kind of like distant relations. There's only one sort of Seafolk like them.'

'Who?'

'The fin-folk,' said Pinch. 'They have a kind of small shark fin on their backs. They're mean and sly and they like nothing better than a nice nibble of flesh. They hide in dark crevices on the seabed, but sometimes they roam about in little boats, hunting for prey. And some of them work as servants for nasty gentry in the deep sea.'

'Yuck,' said Thomas.

'Yuck's right. But what I don't get is this – everyone hates the fin-folk. We don't trust them. So why would Calliope and Pandora go with Peg, if it was to do with them?'

'But it can't be to do with the fin-folk,' said

Thomas. 'Didn't you say Calliope was surprised that Peg brought the message? I think we should wake up Angelica and tell her.'

'Oh no!' said Pinch, nervously.

'Why not?'

'Well, it's ever so late . . .'

'She won't mind, if it's important.'

'But she's going to be ever so mad at me for not telling anyone about the blue moon-clover!' wailed Pinch. 'I didn't even get it in its full strength. I've got to face Mother about that – please, not Angelica as well!'

'OK, let's go and talk to your mother instead,' said Thomas, firmly. 'And Patch, of course.'

Pinch winced, but followed Thomas as they set off. 'She'll be hopping mad that I left her out. I wish we could deal with this ourselves.'

'No. It could be a trap Peg and Nelly set up, with the fin-folk. We must warn the others.'

'Peg and Nelly would never try a stunt like

that,' snorted Pinch. 'They'd be in such trouble! They're Middlers. They couldn't stand being banished. Besides, Calliope and Pandora know how to look after themselves.'

'What if the Uncouthers are mixed up in this?'

They were at the Gulls' door by now. Pinch paused with one hand on the doorknob and stared at him. 'Peg's a nasty piece of work but she's always guarded her waterhole against the Uncouthers. She doesn't like them any more than we do.'

'I just don't think we should rule anything out.'

Pinch sighed. 'I suppose you're right,' he said, glumly.

At that moment, the door flew open, startling them both. Patch stood on the doorstep, hands on her hips. She glared at her brother and Thomas.

'It's not fair! Where have you been! Why didn't you take me with—'

'Look, Patch,' broke in Thomas, 'don't worry about that, for the moment. Is your mum up?'

THREE

Patch knocked on her mother's door, softly. No answer. She knocked again, more loudly. Still no answer.

'We can talk to her in the morning,' said Pinch, relieved.

'It might be too late then,' said Thomas.

Patch stared at them. 'Come on, spit it out. What's all this about?'

They told her. She said, 'I see. I think we'd better tell Mother, even if we have to wake her up . . .'

She turned the handle of the door and slipped into the dark room. She went to the bed. 'Mother . . .' she began, then shouted, 'Oh! Ow!' as she tripped and stumbled over something. She put out a hand to save herself – and yelled, 'She's not here! She's gone!'

Thomas and Pinch tumbled in. Pinch lit the lamp.

'Oh!' they all said together this time. For they could see what Patch had tripped over now. Old Gal usually kept her most valuable dried herbs in a little locked cupboard by her bed. But the cupboard was gaping open, and the neatly-labelled packets of herbs were scattered everywhere. And Old Gal was gone. The bed had been slept in, but the bedclothes were pushed right back, as if the twins' mother had got up in a great hurry.

'Someone's kidnapped her!' wailed Pinch.

'Don't be silly. Her cloak's gone,' said Patch, investigating the wardrobe. 'And she's taken her walking shoes. She must have gone willingly.'

'Did you hear her go, though?' asked Pinch.

'No, but . . .'

'Maybe she went out of the window,'

interrupted Thomas, pulling back the curtains. The window, which gave on to the woods, was slightly open.

'Yes,' said Pinch. 'She probably went out that way.'

Meanwhile, Patch was looking around the room. Suddenly, she held up a piece of paper. 'Look! A note!'

In her spiky hand, Old Gal had written, 'Children: Urgent job. Back in morning. Don't worry. Do chores. Till later, Mother.'

'Typical,' grumbled Pinch. 'Keeps you in suspense – and tells you to do chores!'

'Must have been a very urgent job,' said Thomas, glancing at the mess. Old Gal was usually very neat and tidy about her work.

Patch bent down to pick up some of the scattered packets of herbs. 'Maybe someone got taken really ill and Mother had to go and heal them in the middle of the night.'

'I didn't know people like you – I mean, Hidden Worlders – could get sick,' said Thomas.

Patch stared up at him. 'Of course we can. Not like Obbos – not with disease and bugs and things. But there's poison-magic – the spell sorcerers use if they want to enslave us to do their bidding. It weakens you gradually, till you can't resist. The Uncouthers used to help sorcerers to do it – they'd capture a Hidden Worlder and sell him or her to the sorcerer.'

'How horrid!' said Thomas.

'It hasn't happened for ages, though,' said Pinch. 'That's part of the treaty with the Uncouthers. They're strictly forbidden to traffic in slaves. And also now we have really good relations with most human magicians. They keep an eye on the bad apples for us. They don't want to be banned for ever from the Hidden World!'

Patch was shuffling the herb packets. 'What's missing? It might give us a clue what Mother's doing.' She held them up, one by one. 'Here's sea-change, and fairy-green, and wander-lust, and touch-of-gold and love-at-first-sight . . .

Here's star-bright and fancy-free and mind-wings and—'

'OK, OK,' said Pinch, impatiently. 'But what's missing?'

'I don't know,' said Patch. 'But I think we'd better go and tell Angelica everything, at once.'

'You go,' said Pinch, hurriedly. 'I'll . . . I'll get the blue moon-clover dried, and then at least Mother might be able to use it.'

'Chicken!' said Patch, grinning.

Patch and Thomas hurried down to the café. There was a light on in Angelica's room, right at the top of the building. She responded at once to their quiet knock, and listened carefully to their story. She said, 'You were right to come and see me. This is important. But I do wish Calliope had talked to me first . . .'

'Are they in danger?' said Thomas.

'I don't think so. But this is all highly unusual.'

'You haven't heard any startling news from

the Seafolk, Miss Eyebright?' said Patch, shyly.

'Nothing. Well, apart from the usual thing – quarrels and fights and so on. They're so clannish and proud, that lot. Especially the selkies.'

'The selkies!' said Thomas, remembering a bright selkie girl, Roanna, who with her dolphin friend Delfinus had rescued him from the sea, in the adventure of the Klint-King's gold.

'Yes. There's trouble between the big selkie clans – the Proteans, the Nereans, the Lochlans – but I can't see how any of that would concern us. They're always quarrelling, but they usually sort it out in the end. Hmm.' She smiled at the children. 'You've done exactly the right thing. Thank you for telling me. Now, don't worry. I'll make some inquiries. Hopefully, I'll know by dawn what's going on.' She turned to Patch. 'I'm sure your mother is perfectly all right. She's very sensible and knows exactly what she's doing. Don't worry.

And tell Pinch I'm not cross with him at all.
Now, I think it's time for bed – for everyone.'

FOUR

There was something hot and shining pressing down against Thomas's face. He tried to push it away, but couldn't. He opened his eyes – and found himself lying in bed with the bright sunlight streaming in through the window. He'd been asleep for ages!

He jumped up, got dressed and went downstairs. The café was already busy with customers.

'Well, good afternoon, Thomas!' said his father, Gareth, brightly.

'Is it that late?'

'Joke,' explained his father.

It was good his father was joking again, even

if the jokes were lame Dad-type ones. Gareth had become friendly with a pretty young witch, Lily Lafay, but she wasn't allowed to live permanently in the Hidden World. She had returned to her home in the Obvious World. Since then, Gareth had looked rather glum. Thomas hoped very much that his dad wouldn't suggest they go back to London. He didn't want to return to his old life there. Besides, Lily was OK, but he didn't want anyone trying to take his mum's place.

'It's nearly lunch-time,' went on his father. 'Did you go to a midnight ball, or something?'

Another lame joke. Thomas smiled impatiently. 'Didn't Angelica tell you, Dad?'

'About what? She's gone off on one of her trips.'

'In Metallicus?' Metallicus was the talking car – a very grumpy sort – that belonged to Adverse Camber, the dwarf.

'No, he's out of commission at the moment. She left a note for Adverse.'

'Where is he?'

'Who? Oh, Adverse. He's at Monotype's. Hey, where are you going?'

Monotype Eberhardt was the village bookseller, or keeper of books as it's more generally known in Owlchurch. That's because being a bookseller in the Hidden World is more like being a zoo-keeper than anything. Hidden World books have minds of their own, like animals. Some of them are meek and quiet and gentle, and are happy to browse gently on the shelves, or snooze in the sunlight that streams into the bookshop window. Others are fierce, scratchy little numbers that never want to stay where you put them, and that will suddenly clap open their pages and shout 'Boo!' at an unsuspecting customer. Some of them – especially the bigger, fatter ones – love to hear themselves talk, and will recite all the stories contained within their long, long pages. Others are flighty as flocks of birds, and are constantly flitting about, giggling at their own jokes, and leading poor Monotype quite a dance as he tries to tie them down to their places.

The bookshop is small and cosy, panelled in sweet-smelling cedar, and lined with beautiful old bookshelves. There's also a mezzanine floor halfway up the wall, with a carved wooden balcony all round. Big cabinets with reinforced glass doors line the mezzanine. They're for holding in the most feisty and wild of the books, the kind that will go for your throat or try to bite off your hand or grip you with claws of steel.

Monotype and Adverse Camber were up there, crouching at a cabinet, their backs to Thomas, talking in low voices. Thomas ran up the stairs.

Monotype stood up and dusted himself. He beamed at Thomas. 'Good morning, lad.' He was tall and thin, round yellow eyes blinking like a kindly owl's through his half-moon spectacles. His hair stuck out in grizzled tufts over his ears, and he always wore a shabby black suit with a splendid red polka-dot tie and highly-polished, though never matching, shoes. Next to his long lanky form, Adverse Camber looked smaller and stockier than ever.

'What's up, Thomas?' said the dwarf.

Thomas said, 'Angelica told you what happened.' Adverse nodded. 'And Dad said she's gone off on a trip, but not in Metallicus.'

'That's right,' said Adverse. 'Metallicus is feeling poorly. I must fix his innards. Mind you, I think it's just pure bad temper. No, Angelica went off with Mr Tamblin – worse luck for her,' he added, grimly. There was no love lost between him and the elegant co-mayor of Aspire.

'His car can fly,' explained Monotype.

'Fly? But they need to go to the sea.'

'They've gone to Ariel country – part of it is actually above Seafolk territory. The Ariels keep a bit of a watch on what's happening down there. They might have heard something. Angelica thought it was best to be discreet, at first, just in case it's a storm in a teacup. Seafolk can be touchy. She said she'll be back soon.'

'Oh.'

Adverse turned back to the bookseller. 'Let's get on with it, Monotype.'

'What are you doing?' asked Thomas, curiously.

'Waking up Maldict. The Book of Curses,' said the bookseller. 'Not a very nice book. Not a wild beast, more a snaky sort, you might say. But usually keeps pretty quiet. Sleeps a lot, you know. Hard to wake up. Don't like to do it, much. But no help for it, today.'

Catching Thomas's bewildered expression, Adverse explained, 'Old Gal asked us to do it.'

'Old Gal!'

'It's like this, Thomas. One of the Green Man's henchmen – Bosky – went scouting down on the other side of the forest. Near a remote little wood-stream, he came across an unconscious and very sick nymph. He carried her on his back all the way to the Green Man's headquarters. They tried to nurse her but she got no better so they called Old Gal to help . . . Well, turns out the nymph was poisoned . . .'

'Poisoned?' Thomas's mind flew to what the twins had told him. 'By a sorcerer's spell?'

'Oh no. By a curse,' said Monotype, gravely. 'And not a human sorcerer's curse, either, but one from the Hidden World. Old Gal is sure of that.'

'Uncouthers?'

'Perhaps. Though perhaps not. Old Gal thinks maybe from Mirkengrim. Seafolk badlands. Though she's not sure.'

'That's why we have to wake up this dratted book, so we can investigate,' said Monotype, carefully unlocking the cabinet and opening it.

The books on the shelves were held back by thin gold wires. They looked a disreputable lot, shabby and stained. And they smelled bad, like centuries of mould. They did not make a move, but Thomas felt as if unseen, unfriendly eyes were watching him, and menacing whispers filled the air. He held his breath.

The bookseller reached in behind one of the shelves. Now Thomas could distinctly hear the threatening rattle of pages, and the smell grew stronger. Adverse said, calmly, 'Stand back a little, Thomas. These poison-magic books and sorcerers' diaries aren't very nice types . . . jaws are clamped shut but I wouldn't put it past them to try and spit at you . . .'

Thomas stepped back, but craned his neck to see. Monotype was pulling something out. A covered square basket, patterned in zigzags of black and red. KEEP OUT, read some lettering on the top. Monotype opened the cover cautiously and looked in. He poked in a finger. He said, 'It's fast asleep. I'll have to charm it out.'

Adverse looked up at Thomas. 'Go.'

'Oh, no!' pleaded Thomas. 'Can't I watch?'

Adverse looked like he was about to say no, but Monotype held up a hand. 'It's all right. Maldict will be drowsy and slow. Safe enough, as long as you stay on the stairs, Thomas. But go if I tell you to.'

Excitedly, Thomas nodded.

Monotype closed the door of the cabinet and took an odd little whistle from his pocket. It was bleached white, shaped like a chicken wishbone, with holes down either prong. Very cautiously, he opened the lid of the basket. He put the whistle to his lips. He blew down one prong of the whistle. A long, strange, spooky note came out. It made the hair rise on the back of Thomas's neck, because he thought it sounded like a voice, a high, unearthly voice, whispering, 'Come . . . come . . . come . . .'

Monotype blew the whistle again, the other prong this time. Now the note sounded long and deep and booming, like the voice of some undersea thing. 'Come . . . come . . . come,' it boomed, and as the note died away, suddenly Thomas heard something else – like dry scales rasping against straw. Something was moving around, in the basket!

Cold gripped Thomas's spine. Terror invaded him. He suddenly wanted to run away, but couldn't move. Monotype blew once more, down both prongs of the whistle. And he kept blowing. The two notes played together, in, out, in, out, a note of terrible calling. And then Thomas saw something appear at the lip of the basket. Something of a strange, horrible colour, pale and ghostly, with a big, blind, questing head. A shapeless book whose binding hung baggy on it, like a sea snake's skin, a book from which came the stink of rotting things. A page flapped open, lazily. Maldict swayed drowsily in time to Monotype's strange tune, and Thomas found himself swaying in time too. His hand left the rail; it hung limply at his side. He swayed. He could hear a voice in his head, 'Come . . .

come . . . my sweet . . . my pretty . . . you come . . . come . . . come home . . .'

'Thomas!' Adverse leaped forward, catching him just as he was about to faint. Monotype hastily took the whistle from his lips. Maldict's head moved, searching. The bookseller quickly slammed the lid of the basket down. The book disappeared at once.

Adverse growled, 'Some people! I told you it was dangerous!'

'You'd better go, Thomas,' said the bookseller.

Thomas felt shaky. His head was spinning. He wasn't at all sure what had happened. For an instant, he remembered a kind of black fog and a sweet, sinister voice. The next, it had gone. He faltered, 'I'm OK, now, really I am. I want to see what you—'

'No way,' said Adverse, firmly marching him down the stairs. 'No arguing. You go. You're brave and clever, Thomas, but you're no match for Maldict. Oh, and fetch Hinkypunk for us, won't you? I think we're going to need his help.'

FIVE

Hinkypunk Hobthrust was sitting on the doorstep of his Tricks shop. He grinned his foxy grin as Thomas approached. 'Well, hello, if it isn't our True Tom without his faithful twin shadows! What's up, eh – a little tiff?'

Thomas didn't feel like arguing. Hinkypunk could be a lot of fun but he also loved to make stinging remarks, and stir trouble. You never quite knew where you were with him. 'You're wanted at the bookshop, Mr Hobthrust. Monotype and Adverse need your help.'

Hinkypunk raised his red eyebrows. 'Difficult customer, eh? What sort of book is it, may I ask?'

'It's Maldict,' said Thomas, and at the sound of the name, he shivered. He could see the book in his mind's eye, the snaky, unpleasant way it moved, the blind questing head, the smell . . . ugh! He hoped he'd never have to see it ever again.

Hinkypunk watched him with bright, gleeful eyes. 'Maldict, eh! Well, well. I haven't clapped eyes on Maldict for quite some time. Years and years in fact. It'll be a pleasure, matching wits with that wicked old rogue again. Well, well! Fancy dear old Adverse asking little old me to help with Maldict. I always thought he was of the opinion it should be weighted down with a stone and drowned, at the very least.' His bright amber eyes searched Thomas's face. 'Trouble in paradise, eh? Must be something serious, if Maldict's been dragged out.' He looked sharply at Thomas. 'You look a little green around the gills, my lad. Maldict's enough to put anyone off his breakfast. Fancy Monotype letting you take a look! Getting soft in his old age, eh!'

'No, no, I asked to watch,' said Thomas, and fled before Hinkypunk could say any more. Sometimes the Trickster made him feel very uncomfortable indeed.

He found his friends in the Gull cottage kitchen, Patch chopping herbs and Pinch washing up an army of little bottles.

'There you are at last!' cried Pinch. 'Did you hear about Mother and the nymph?'

Thomas flung himself into a chair. 'Yes. I've just come from the bookshop. There's this book of curses they were tackling . . .' He hesitated. 'The book goes by the name of Maldict.' It was OK. He could say the name without feeling weird now.

Pinch and Patch shot a glance at each other. 'Oh, that one,' said Patch. 'It was compiled by the Uncouthers long ago. It was one of the things that was captured from them when there was that war with them. They were furious at its loss, but they've never managed to get hold of it again. I'm sure they'd love to, though.'

'Oh, I see.' Thomas thought, that was why Maldict made me feel bad. 'So Maldict is full of Uncouther curses?'

'Not just them. There's curses from all the parts of the Hidden World, as well as a few human ones.'

'Oh, right.'

'Did they tell you much about the nymph?' said Pinch.

'No. Who is she?'

'She's a wood-stream nymph. A sweetwater girl, of course. But there's bitter water in this one's veins. And there shouldn't be.'

'Bitter water?'

'Salt water,' explained Patch. 'Nymphs usually have clear, sweet water in their veins. They don't go near the sea. But this girl had bitter water in *her* veins. And Mother thinks that there's no way that bitter water got into her unless she was cursed. Or her stream was, which comes to the same thing.'

'What does she say about it?'

'She can't speak,' Pinch said. He waved a hand at the piles of herbs. 'These are to heal her. But it'll all take time, even with a bit of the blue moon-clover added. It still works,' he added proudly.

'Right! That must be the news Peg brought – I mean, about the nymph,' Thomas said.

Pinch shook his head. 'Mother says not.'

'But if she thinks the curse comes from Mirkengrim...'

'That's just one possibility. There's worse. The Uncouthers are up to no good.'

'You see,' explained Patch, 'that stream is remote. And nymphs aren't fierce like Peg Powler. It's a good place to test out a weak spot.'

'You mean they're trying to come up through the stream?' breathed Thomas.

'No. Worse. You see, that stream runs into another, then a river, and so on. If you poison the stream and its keeper with a curse – and

38

she dies – then the bitter water in her body will flow into those other streams. Then everything near them would die,' said Patch, solemnly. 'And the Uncouthers would have a clear run. Who could stop them invading?'

'I thought they weren't going to do anything like that any more!' cried Thomas.

Patch shrugged. 'Things can change very easily down there. You know what?' she went on, deftly packing the herbs into little paper bags. 'I think we should take these directly to Mother. Don't you?'

They looked at each other. 'Absolutely!' said Thomas and Pinch, together.

SIX

Soon they were at the great twisted tree that was the Green Man's home and hideout. It was an amazing sight, very tall and wide, with leaves of all colours on it, as if every season was happening at once. Acorn, Bosky and Skrob, the Green Man's bushy-haired and bearded sidekicks, were just outside, playing cards and keeping watch.

'Hello, kids,' said Bosky, gruffly, without looking up from his card-game. 'Hang on, Skrob – you can't do that!' he yelled, as Skrob threw down a winning hand.

'I can too,' said Skrob, smugly, gathering all the cards up and the little pile of acorn-cups

they used as winnings. 'You're just a bad loser, Bosky.'

'And you're a cheat,' sneered Bosky.

'Say that again and I'll clock you one,' shouted Skrob.

Acorn snapped, 'Stop it, both of you. You're making fools of yourselves. You come to see your mum and dad?' he added, to the twins. 'The Green Man's gone to have another look at the stream, but your mum's with that poor nymph. Go right in. Now then, Skrob, Bosky, let's have another game, shall we?'

Three times, Pinch rapped on the trunk of the tree. Then, with a grinding, tearing sound, it opened, revealing a dimly-lit passageway beyond. The children stepped in, while the door closed slowly behind them.

The passage led to the main room of the tree-house. It was lovely, big and airy, decorated in shades of green and gold. And it was empty, except for a still figure lying on the soft cushions in a corner. The figure was small, wrapped in a shapeless brown robe, with a soft green quilt drawn up to its waist. The hair was an odd colour: a kind of dull greeny-yellow, short and lank as waterweed. The face was pointed and sharp, the skin greyish and peeling in long strips, showing a raw-looking whiteness underneath. The mouth and eyes were closed, and long eyelashes of the same dull colour as the hair lay on the peeling cheeks. There was a faint smell about her, the smell of stagnant water.

'Poor thing,' said Patch, softly. 'She looks almost dead.'

'Patch Gull! Don't say such things,' said her mother's voice, and Old Gal walked into the room. Pinch and Patch launched into a flood of explanations at once, but Old Gal cut them short.

'I'm glad you're here. Give me those herbs.' She took the basket from them. 'I was hoping she'd look better by now but she seems to have had a relapse. I'll mix up some super-strength ones. If you want to make yourselves useful, just sit here and watch her. She may wake up at any moment. You must be quiet.'

Old Gal went out. The children settled themselves on the cushions. At first they were very quiet, watching the still, grey face of the girl. But soon they grew bored. Pinch got up and ran around the room. When Patch told him to be quiet, he picked up a cushion and threw it at his sister. She jumped up and threw another one at him. Thomas told them both to stop. In reply, Pinch threw a cushion at him. It was Thomas's turn to jump up, and lob a cushion at his friend. They were careful not to go anywhere near the girl, but they were making a fair bit of racket, so much so that at first they didn't hear the quiet little gurgle of sound.

But the second time, Thomas heard it. He turned around in a flash. The girl had woken up. She was staring straight at him. A lightning bolt of shock hit him as he looked into her eyes. He cried, 'Oh, no! Oh, *no!*'

'What's the matter?' said Patch, startled.

'She . . . she . . .' Thomas pointed with a shaking finger at the girl. 'She's not . . . not . . .'

'Not what?' faltered Pinch. 'What's up with you?'

'Look . . . look . . .' stammered Thomas. 'She's not . . . not a nymph!'

'What do you mean?' cried Patch.

Thomas dropped down to his knees near the girl. He took one of her cold grey hands. He looked into the dull, hopeless eyes which had once been so bright. He whispered, 'Oh, poor Roanna, what's happened to you?'

Together, Pinch and Patch said, 'What?'

Thomas held Roanna's hand. He whispered, 'This is Roanna of the Protean clan, the selkie girl who rescued me from the sea, with her friend Delfinus . . .'

'The selkie girl?' breathed Patch, dropping to her knees too. She stared at the sick girl. 'But I don't understand . . . Why didn't Mother know . . . I mean, everyone knows what selkies are like. How could she think she's a nymph?'

Thomas took no notice. He bent down and whispered, 'You *are* Roanna, aren't you? Nod if you are.'

'She's paralysed, Thomas,' said Patch, sadly. 'She can't nod, or anything. It's just her eyes that can move.'

'Blink, then,' said Thomas, desperately. 'Blink twice if it's you, Roanna.'

The girl blinked, slowly, painfully. Once. And then, after a moment, once more.

'I'm going to get Mother,' said Pinch, excitedly, and rushed off.

'But what happened to her?' said Patch, softly.

Thomas shook his head. It had to be something really awful, to put Roanna in such a terrible state. And why hadn't everyone known she was a selkie from the start? How could they make that mistake?

'It's all right, Roanna,' he whispered. 'You're safe and among friends, and you'll get better. We'll make you better. You'll see. You'll soon be all right. You will, I promise.'

How he was going to fulfil that promise, he didn't know. But he had to try.

SEVEN

'It certainly explains why she's not getting better,' said Old Gal. 'I've been giving her the wrong sort of medicines.' She picked up Roanna's limp hand. The girl had fainted again. 'But it's really strange. When Vertome' – that was the Green Man's name – 'found her, she was clad in nymph's costume – white draperies, rather torn and muddy, and a crown of waterweed on her head. There was nothing, but *nothing*, to show she was a selkie. No little cap, no second skin – you know, that sealskin they wear – and no smell of the sea. Only her hair seemed a little short for a nymph. But I can't say I took much notice of that. She was much too sick . . .' She straightened up. 'I must get home and fetch some more things. Pinch and Patch, come with me. Thomas, could you stay with Roanna?'

'Of course,' said Thomas, seating himself beside the girl. 'I won't budge, I promise!'

'Can't we stay, too?' said Patch.

'No,' said Old Gal, firmly. 'I need you to help me get stuff ready quickly and carry it here. Now, Thomas. We'll be back soon. In the meantime, if she wakes up, put a little of this on her tongue.' She took out a little bottle from her apron pocket and handed it to him, as well as a tiny dropper. 'Here's the blue moon-clover I've been able to salvage. In solution like this it's safe for all water-people and it should help a little, until we get back with the more powerful stuff.'

Left alone, Thomas sat and watched Roanna. He felt scared and sad. Would Roanna recover, or might she die? He had never thought he'd see someone die, in this world. He'd never even thought they might die. Come to think of it, he'd just assumed Hidden Worlders must be immortal. But perhaps they just lived much, much longer than human beings. After all, he remembered seeing, in the palace of Reidmar Redbeard, the Klint-King, portraits of Reidmar's ancestors, who'd been Kings and Queens before him. That must mean they had died, or at least vanished somehow. It wasn't something he'd ever wondered about, before.

His eyes filled with tears. He'd never thought they could get sick, either – and yet here was Roanna, so sick she looked almost dead. Yet when he'd last seen her, she had been so joyful and full of life, turning somersaults in the bright sea air! The Hidden World still held many surprises for him – and not all good ones, apparently.

'Poor Roanna,' he whispered, and a tear fell on to the girl's cheek. Then another. And another. Thomas tried to stop crying, but he couldn't. It seemed unbearable to him that the girl who had been so much at home in the sea should be in danger of death, so far from home. Somebody had done this to her! Somebody horrible and cruel who had poisoned her with a wicked curse, for whatever deep and ugly reason Thomas didn't know, and didn't care. Whoever that somebody was, I'll find them and punish them, he thought, fiercely, as the tears kept falling. I don't care if it is the Uncouthers – I'm not scared, I'm going to get them for this!

All at once, he noticed something. The girl's face was changing. Or rather, the colour of her skin was. The peels of dull skin vanished, the raw-looking skin was healing over, the grey went to white then pale green then to the silvery glow Thomas remembered from before. The silver seemed to spread up her forehead, into her hairline, and as Thomas watched in startled amazement, her hair began to change colour too, turning bright in stages, as if dozens of little lights were being switched on, one after the other. As he watched, his tears drying, his heart full of stunned joy, the brightness spread all the way up and down the selkie girl's body. Her eyes opened and she looked straight at Thomas. Roanna's eyes weren't quite as bright as the first time Thomas had seen them, but they were a long way from the dull hopelessness of the sick girl.

'Oh, Roanna!' Thomas whispered. 'You're awake. You look better . . .' His heart was beating fast. What had happened? Was it something to do with his tears, falling on her skin?

Roanna opened her mouth and tried to speak. But no sound came out. She looked desperately at Thomas, and gestured at her throat.

'Wait a moment, wait a moment,' gabbled Thomas, scrambling for the little bottle of blue moon-clover mixture, and drawing up a bit of it into the dropper. Gently, he put a little drop, then another and another, on the girl's tongue. A gurgling sound came from her, louder than before. More gurgles. Thomas waited anxiously. Would it work?

Roanna's body gave a great jerk. Her hands clutched at the quilt. A croak came from her throat. She tried again. At last, she managed to gasp, 'Help . . . help me sit . . .'

Thomas's heart turned a cartwheel of relief. 'Do you want to sit up?'

She nodded. Thomas piled some cushions behind her back and gently helped her sit up. She grimaced, and touched her throat. 'Hurts . . . hurts . . .'

Thomas picked up the bottle of mixture. She shook her head. 'No . . . no . . . not yet . . .'

'Old Gal will be coming soon,' said Thomas, nervously. 'She'll know what to do, for your throat. Oh, Roanna, what happened to you?'

She smiled faintly. 'Came . . . to get you.'

'Me?' said Thomas, even more nervously. 'What for?'

'You know . . .' Her voice changed, and turned into a croak again. She put a hand

to her throat. Tears suddenly sprang into her eyes.

'Don't worry,' said Thomas, very anxiously now. 'They'll soon be here.' Oh, hurry, hurry, hurry, he thought. In her shapeless robe, fastened on her with big pins, Roanna looked very small and thin. She held out a trembling hand, and he took it. 'It's all right,' he repeated.

'Hurts . . .' she whispered.

He patted her hand, not knowing what else to do. Suddenly, she grabbed at his arm. 'Go . . . go . . . must go . . .'

'Go? Are you crazy? No way. You must stay here till my friends get back.'

'No . . . go . . . go . . .' croaked Roanna. She gulped, swallowed, and with a huge effort, got more words out.

'Must . . . go . . . or . . . too late . . . you . . .' She poked a finger at Thomas's chest. 'You . . . go . . . with me . . .'

'Me?' said Thomas. 'You want me to go with you? But where?'

She looked a little panicky. 'But you . . . you . . . know . . . go . . . home . . .'

'Your home? That's why you came to get me?' She nodded, vigorously.

'But you were a long way from Owlchurch when you—'

'Lost,' she blurted. 'Lost way . . . sorry . . . please . . . please . . . you come . . . now . . .'

'I can go with you if you like,' said Thomas, carefully, because he didn't want her to get more upset. 'But not right now. You can't walk, and I'm not strong like Bosky, I can't carry you. Besides, where would we go? We're nowhere near the sea here, not even near the river. We're deep in the forest. We've got to wait till the others come back and then work out what to do.'

She stared at him, her eyes huge. Then to Thomas's relief she nodded, rather glumly. She said, 'But you—' But before she could attempt to finish her sentence, there was the sound of running feet down the passage. In the next instant, Pinch appeared, Patch hot on his heels.

EIGHT

We've got all the—' Pinch began, excitedly, but he stopped dead as he saw Roanna sitting up. Patch was so astonished that she dropped the basket of herbs she was holding and had to scramble to pick it all up.

'What . . . what . . . how . . .' stammered Pinch.

'I don't know,' said Thomas. 'Not really.' He felt rather shy about saying he had cried. 'Anyway, Roanna, here are my friends – Pinch and Patch Gull. Do you remember them from . . .'

Roanna nodded. She tried to say 'Hello.' It came out more like a kind of throat-clearing.

At that moment, Old Gal came in. She did a

double-take when she saw them. 'Great Pan!' she cried, and hurried to Roanna's side. She took her hand. She listened to her chest. An odd expression came over her thin face. She said, 'How amazing. How utterly amazing.' She looked at Thomas. 'Suppose you tell us what happened,' she said, gently.

When Thomas had finished, everyone was quiet. Then Old Gal sighed and said, in a soft, wondering sort of voice, 'Well, I've heard of such a thing happening – that is, I've read about it – but I've never seen it myself, before. You see, Thomas, human tears are not only salty – and she needed her salt levels up – it's like the breath of life to her – but also, there is something special, something magical, about the tears of our human friends. They can sometimes help to bring Hidden Worlders from the very brink of death. It doesn't always work, mind you – it can't be relied on. But when it does work, it is a magic as great as our own.'

'Oh,' said Thomas, sheepish and thrilled at the same time. Pinch and Patch were looking at him as if they'd never seen him before, and it made him feel odd. 'I . . . I didn't know that.'

'No reason why you would,' said Old Gal, the briskness back in her voice. 'Now, did you give her the clover, too?'

Roanna opened her mouth. 'Yes,' she croaked.

Old Gal put her head to one side. 'Hmm. Still a problem there, I think . . .' She knelt by Roanna and listened first to her chest, then to her throat. 'As I thought. A little intruder. Pinch and Patch, hand me the star-bright and sea-change, for a start. And give me the mortar and pestle. I'll grind it all up right here.' She rolled up her sleeves and set to work crushing and blending the herbs, adding a little drop of some silver liquid. 'Thomas – hand me the spoon. Yes, the silver one with the dolphin's head on it. Roanna, open your mouth wide.'

The mixture went in. Roanna made a face. 'I

know,' said Old Gal, 'it tastes nasty. But it'll get rid of— Ah! There it goes!' she said, as something small and shadowy leaped from Roanna's mouth. It jumped like a frog, but its outline was blurred, and it was transparent. 'The stream-frog, I rather think,' said Old Gal, cupping a swift hand over the little thing. She opened a bottle and shoved it in, corking the bottle up immediately. 'It's the stream-spirit, and only trying to protect its patch. Now, dear,' she went on, turning to Roanna, 'does that feel better?'

Roanna opened her mouth. She said, 'I . . . I think so.' Her voice did seem a good deal better, more normal.

Thomas stared at the bottle. He couldn't see the frog properly, only catch its frantic movements as it flung itself against the glass. He said, 'Was that what made Roanna sick?'

'Having it in her throat gave her sweetwater-sickness, but she was already feeling poorly, weren't you, dear?'

Roanna nodded. She said, 'We all are.' Her voice was much stronger now.

'All, dear?'

'My clan. We've all been a bit unwell. That's why I came. Delfinus – he said Thomas would help.' She looked pleadingly at Thomas. But he had no idea what she was talking about.

'They wouldn't listen,' she added.

Old Gal looked bewildered. 'Who?'

'My grandmother – and the other elders. They told me to mind my own business, that a human stranger, no matter how clever he was, couldn't solve things for us. So I decided I had to run away and get Thomas myself, and—'

'How did you disguise yourself so well?' interrupted Old Gal. 'No one knew you were a selkie.'

'Good, wasn't I? I studied how nymphs talked and swam and so on . . . and also, well, you see, I went to Oceanopolis,' said Roanna, proudly. 'You can get most anything there . . .'

'For a price,' said Old Gal, grimly.

Roanna looked uneasy. 'Yes, well – for a price. But I'll get it back and . . .'

'You pawned your second skin and your cap, didn't you, child?' said Old Gal, even more grimly. 'You went to a sea-witch and asked her for a potion to help you breathe in sweet water, and look like a nymph, isn't that so?'

'How do you know that?' said Roanna, staring.

'I know that selkies can breathe salt water and air, but not sweet water,' shrugged Old Gal. 'I know only strong magic can change that. It follows that you must have gone to a sea-witch. But what you did was crazy, my girl. Whatever the witch told you, no sea-thing can breathe sweet water for long. It makes you sick very quickly. What's more, giving up your second skin and cap will make it very hard for you to go home.'

'I didn't give up my cap,' snapped Roanna. 'Every selkie knows you must never give that up or you can never return to the sea. I hid it –

buried it on the beach where I landed. And what's more I took another one for Thomas. As to my second skin, I'm going to redeem it as soon as I get home. Grandmother will give me the money. She won't be happy, but she will give it to me.'

Old Gal snorted. 'Foolish child! There's a black market in such things and they fetch high prices. It's likely the witch has sold it in Mirkengrim. It might even end up in Nightmare. You'll never see it again.'

'Oh yes I will,' said Roanna, stubbornly. 'The witch promised she'd keep it.'

'And you believed her!'

'She'll lose her licence if she doesn't keep her promise,' said Roanna, haughtily. 'I am from a leading selkie family. She won't want to lose our custom.'

Old Gal looked as though she wanted to give Roanna a good scolding. But before she could speak, Thomas hastily butted in. 'Roanna, was it the curse that's weakened your clan?'

Roanna brightened. 'You see!' she said, with a defiant glance at Old Gal. 'I was right to come! Thomas already knows what's happening! That's why he—'

'What kind of curse?' said Old Gal, sharply. 'Who called it? Uncouthers? Mirkengrim?'

Roanna's eyes widened. She shot a look at Thomas that he couldn't understand. She said, 'Oh, no! It was the Lochlan clan. It's revenge for stealing a new tune of theirs. Or at least they claim we stole it.'

'And did you?'

Roanna looked a bit shifty. 'Of course not! We have much better tunes than the Lochlans, anyway, and if someone should make up a new tune that had never been heard before – well, that's because we're clever, not because we're thieves! But the thing is, they thought it was true. They claimed that this new tune was a deep secret of theirs. And so in a fit of fury one of them – we don't yet know which one – called down the Cacophony Curse on us.'

'The Cacophony Curse?' said Old Gal.

'It's a very old and very horrid one, made up centuries ago by a wicked selkie who had been banished from our country. It weakens your ear. You can no longer tell the difference between melody and noise, between harmony and discord. Every tune sounds horrible to you. You don't dare to play or to open your mouth to sing. And because music runs in our veins like the sea, not being able to sing and play weakens us day by day.'

'A nasty punishment for musicians, I can see that.'

'But the curse is very dangerous, because it's very hard to control. It spreads like wildfire. All the selkie clans will catch it, and then the rest of the Seafolk . . . And then, if it's not stopped, the curse will get into all the music streams, everywhere in the Hidden World. Every song, every tune will die. There will only be horrible noise – or endless silence.'

No one spoke. Then Old Gal said, 'What I

don't understand is this – if it's so dangerous, why in Pan's name would the Lochlans have called it down? They stand to lose as much by it as you do.'

'That's just it. They swear it *wasn't* them,' said Roanna. 'But our elders don't believe them. The Lochlans were overheard threatening to call the curse, you see. There's no doubt about that. And no one else could call it. I mean, only a selkie could call it. And only the Lochlans, of all the selkie clans, have the motive.'

Old Gal sighed. 'Oh dear. So that was the message Nelly Long Arms brought, I suppose.'

Roanna nodded. 'Yes.' Again, she shot that puzzled, puzzling look at Thomas. 'The elders were silly to ignore the fact that Delfinus had got—'

'You shouldn't talk like that about your elders,' interrupted Old Gal, sternly. 'Their message reached us safely – two of our people have already left for your country.'

'Oh,' said Roanna. She looked at Thomas.

'Why won't you tell them?'

'Tell what?' said Thomas, bewildered.

'You promised you'd come!' snapped Roanna. 'You promised!'

The twins glared at Thomas, who went red. He said, feebly, 'I didn't *promise*. I just said maybe after the others get back and . . .'

Old Gal raised her eyebrows. Turning to Roanna, she said, 'You are a rash and silly girl. You did a very dangerous thing, and very nearly paid for it with your life.'

'But Thomas...' Roanna began.

'You owe your life not only to Thomas, but to all the rest of us,' said Old Gal, sharply. To Bosky, especially, who found you near that stream. What can you have been thinking of! It's hardly near Owlchurch!'

Roanna looked sulky. 'I lost my way. I went down the wrong bend of the river, that's all.'

'It's not the only mistake you made,' snapped Old Gal. 'Trusting a sea-witch and pawning your second skin was another. As to hiding the cap, well, how do you know it's still there on the beach and that someone hasn't stolen it? Yes, you may well look shocked. Bad things happen. I'm afraid, my dear, we're not going to send Thomas into danger just because you say he must come with you. You're going to have to cool your heels a little till we come to a decision. Is that clearly understood?'

Roanna gulped. She looked totally crestfallen. 'Yes,' she murmured.

Thomas caught the look of glee on the twins' faces. His heart sank. He liked all of them. If only they could all be friends . . .

NINE

It was a silent party that made its way back to Owlchurch. Because Roanna was still rather weak, Bosky and Skrob carried her on a stretcher made of sticks and leaves. Old Gal stayed with them, while the twins forged on ahead. Thomas lagged in the middle, feeling uneasy and uncomfortable and quite annoyed as well. He was annoyed with Pinch and Patch for being so snarky, and with Roanna for just assuming things of him. But deep inside him, he hoped that he'd be allowed to go with her. It would be amazing to see the underwater realms. But he'd want the twins with him. They were his friends. His best friends . . .

He hastened his pace, and caught up with Pinch and Patch.

'Well, hello. Selkie girl send you to tell us something?' said Pinch, coolly.

'Please,' said Thomas, 'please stop getting all shirty about nothing.'

'I thought that was you,' said Pinch, very coldly indeed. 'We haven't done anything, have we, Patch?'

Patch said nothing. Thomas exploded. 'You're acting as if I wasn't your friend any more. You're just jealous, and there's no reason for it. Roanna's nice, but you two are my best friends. My best friends, don't you get it!'

'*She* doesn't,' said Patch, speaking at last. Her voice sounded small and sad. 'You like her a lot. You cried over her and healed her . . .'

'I didn't know that was going to happen!'

'Yes but you did it. You've never cried over us.'

'Don't be silly. You've never needed it,' said Thomas, crossly. 'She looked so terrible . . .

she looked like she was going to die . . . I was really upset . . .'

'And she can live both in the Hidden World and the Obvious World, like you,' went on Patch, as if he hadn't spoken.

'What do you mean?'

'Selkies are sort of like Rymers. Not exactly, but they have human blood in them, way back, so they are also a link between the worlds,' whispered Patch. 'We saw the way she looked at you and we just know she's going to take you away from us and—'

'As if I'd let her!' said Thomas, fiercely. 'I want to help her – yes – but I want you to help me, too. We've got to stick together, the three of us. Only together can we work it out. We always have done, every time, haven't we?'

There was a little silence. Then Pinch said, carefully, 'You really want us to come with you? Into the lands of the Seafolk?'

'Of course,' said Thomas.

'*She* won't want us to,' said Patch.

'Who cares? She'll have to do what she's told.' He felt a squirm of shame as he said that, but it seemed to do the trick. The twins' faces brightened.

'She will, won't she?' said Pinch, gleefully.

'Of course that's supposing Angelica and Mother and your dad and all of them let us go anyway,' said Patch, thoughtfully.

'They'll have to!' exclaimed Pinch. 'Do you think – do you think we'll be able to go to Oceanopolis?' he breathed. 'They say it's a huge city, really amazing . . .'

'Don't see why not,' said Thomas, confidently.

'But Calliope and Pandora might have sorted it out already,' said Patch. 'There might be nothing for us to do.'

'You heard Roanna,' said Pinch. 'She said Delfinus said Thomas was needed and . . .'

'So you're listening to *her* now?' said Patch.

Pinch shrugged. 'Well . . . if Thomas thinks she's right, then . . .'

'But I don't know,' said Thomas, the unease returning. 'I have no idea why Delfinus said I was needed. I hardly know him at all. I only met him, and Roanna, once.' If only the twins hadn't taken so against Roanna! And if only Roanna knew when to shut her mouth! Oh, it was all so difficult!

They came into the village quite a way ahead of Old Gal and the others, and saw the Aspire Mayors' beautiful white limousine, drawn up outside the Apple Tree Café.

Angelica and Mr Tamblin were sitting at a table in the café, with Gareth and Hinkypunk and Monotype and Adverse. They were arguing. Gareth was the first to see the children. He jumped up, his anxious face clearing.

'For goodness' sake, Thomas, you shouldn't run off like that! I was worried . . .'

'Surely not,' drawled Mr Tamblin. He was well-groomed and elegant as ever, in his trademark black suit and cravat. 'How can you

73

worry when it's our dear Thomas, who's always got out of every scrape he's found himself in?'

It didn't sound like a real compliment – everything Mr Tamblin and Lady Pandora said was always edged with a double meaning. Thomas still didn't know if the elegant Aspirants actually liked him or simply put up with him. He wasn't sure what he thought of them either, mind you!

Ignoring Mr Tamblin, Angelica said, 'Where's Old Gal? And how's that girl?'

'They're coming,' said Pinch. 'And she's fine.'

'She pawned her second skin,' said Patch.

'She wanted to find Thomas,' said Pinch.

'Did she now? Thomas, what do you know about this?'

'I don't know anything,' cried Thomas, as everyone looked at him. 'I really don't. I just realised it was her when she opened her eyes.'

'You're sure you didn't send her a message?' said Angelica.

Thomas stared at her. 'No.'

Mr Tamblin waved a languid hand. 'Trouble is, dear boy, we were told by the Ariels that a message was sent to the dolphin Delfinus. *By you*. Well, by a Rymer, anyway. And as you're the only Rymer we know of living in the Hidden World at the moment, it must be you.'

Now the twins looked accusingly at Thomas. He flushed. 'Well, it wasn't! I didn't send a message to anyone!'

Angelica's narrow green eyes looked sharply at him. 'Thomas, it's OK, we're not angry with you, but you must tell us the truth.'

'But I have!' cried Thomas.

'You didn't write to the dolphin and tell him you could help them solve their problem?'

Thomas was thunderstruck. 'Even if I could do anything about something I didn't even know about, how on earth *could* I write to him? I have no idea how to write in dolphin, and I don't know his address. I met him just the once.' At least now Roanna's attitude was making sense. She thought he *had* written to her, or at least to the dolphin, and was puzzled that he didn't mention it. 'Oh dear! I suppose that's why she did it.'

Mr Tamblin raised a sleek eyebrow, and gave a faint smile. 'But of course.'

Thomas went scarlet. Shuffling his feet, he stammered, 'Well, it's not my fault, and I didn't write the note, and I don't know what's happened – and how could I possibly know anything about it and what can I possibly do and . . .'

'But you're right – or whoever sent that message is quite right,' said Monotype, hastily. 'It's in Maldict, you know, that book of curses. The only other time this curse has been called, it was undone by a Rymer. In fact, by the original Rymer, True Thomas himself.'

'So you said,' said Mr Tamblin, 'but Maldict doesn't always tell the truth, you know that. And it didn't explain *how* he undid the curse, did it?'

'Nothing definite,' said Monotype. 'You

know what Uncouther books are like. They hate the idea of doing any good. All it would say was that True Thomas realised that just as music is the food of life for selkies, so noise is their poison. And that just as food is cooked in a pot by the cook, so poison is added to the pot by the poisoner.'

'Is the curse a potion then?' said Angelica.

'Oh no. It's just that Maldict likes to talk in mysteries and metaphors. They make it feel important. I agree it sometimes evades truth. But I felt we should listen to what it said. Maybe only a Rymer can stop this curse. After all, Rymers hear and see things other people can't.'

'But Thomas *didn't* send the message. He knows nothing about it. Someone else sent it,' said Angelica. 'And we don't know who it was. I tell you, I don't like it – any of it, and—'

She broke off as the door opened, and Old Gal and Roanna stood framed in the doorway, the girl leaning on the woman.

TEN

'The boys went home,' said Old Gal, helping the selkie girl to a chair. 'Said to send you their best regards, but that it was hunting time.'

Roanna had one of Bosky's old cloaks over the shapeless robe now and looked smaller than ever. She smiled shyly around.

'Now listen, my girl,' said Angelica, firmly. 'What's this I hear, about a message sent to you? Tell us the truth, now! Did you make it up?'

Roanna looked at Thomas. 'Tell them!'

'Tell them what?'

'But, Thomas, you wrote to me!' cried Roanna, looking hurt and puzzled.

'Look, it *wasn't* me who wrote to Delfinus,' said

Thomas, desperately. 'Where's the message? We'll soon see if it's in my handwriting or not.'

'But you said . . . the message said to destroy the note once I'd read it,' said Roanna, staring. 'So I did.'

'Well, I promise you, Roanna, it wasn't me,' said Thomas.

'But the message was signed "the Rymer", and you're the only Rymer Delfinus and I have ever met, so . . .'

'It could have been anyone!' cried Thomas. 'Some other Rymer, or someone pretending to be one!'

'But why?'

'I don't know. But I can guess. To lure you out – to get you to come here – and to die.'

Roanna stared. 'But who would want to kill me? What for? I'm not an important selkie, or anything . . .'

'Maybe it was to make your clan angry,' said Angelica. 'To set up a problem between Middlers and selkies . . .'

Thomas said, thoughtfully, 'Did this message – did it tell you how to get here?'

'Yes. It had a map,' said Roanna. 'It showed where the river branches, and the streams to follow to get to Owlchurch. Very nice, clear map.'

'Definitely not me! I can't draw maps for anything,' said Thomas, smiling. 'I always get into trouble in geography lessons at school because of it.'

'I think now that the map told me the wrong way to go,' said Roanna, slowly.

'This gets worse and worse,' said Angelica, grimly. 'I am very concerned indeed. A cruel curse – a pretend Rymer – a deadly map – and the Lochlans claiming they never did it.'

'Oh, but they would say that,' said Roanna. 'They know their name would be mud if they admitted to it!'

'It already is, dear girl, after what's happened,' said Mr Tamblin, taking out a little gold file and buffing his already perfect nails.

'Oh, I expect they're ashamed now and wish they hadn't called it, but it's too late,' said Roanna, carelessly.

'Yes, but even if – for the sake of argument – the Lochlans did call the curse – why would they send a message from a fake Rymer?' said Adverse.

Roanna shrugged. 'I just know Thomas will be able to work it all out. I've heard all about the things he's done, like helping with the Klint-King, and with Lord Pan, and even down below . . .' she shuddered, '. . . in Nightmare. I think he's the best person to find out who did this and how to stop it. Don't you?'

'My hero,' mouthed Pinch sarcastically.

Roanna glared around them. 'Oh! I thought you'd understand! I didn't realise you'd all just be as stuffy as Grandmother and the other elders. You just want to go on the same old tracks, doing just what you've always done and never trying anything new.'

'Roanna of the Protean Clan!' Angelica

sounded very stern. 'This kind of talk will cease at once. It is you who does not understand. Thomas is indeed a very brave and clever Rymer – one of the best we've had in a long time. And it's true that we have learned there is a possibility a Rymer stopped just such a curse, long ago. But what you are asking him to do is very, very dangerous. You are a sea-creature; he is not.'

'He will have the cap that I—'

'It's not breathing in seawater that worries me,' broke in Angelica. 'That can be dealt with. But the sea is a huge and ambiguous realm. We can't be sure who's watching and listening. Roanna, did you tell anyone else about the message you supposedly got from Thomas?'

Roanna looked sheepish. 'Well, no. The message said I must not tell anyone, on any account. I did *mention* to Grandmother that perhaps we should get a Rymer, on account of that first time the curse was called, and she just got mad with me, said I didn't know what I was talking about, that the Rymer back then hadn't solved it, he'd just given them advice. She said it was bad enough we had to call on Middler strangers for help, but she'd have no humans meddling in this, thank you very much. Well, then I thought it would be our secret, Delfinus and I, that we'd go and fetch Thomas, and we'd solve it all together and everyone would know it was us who did it, and they'd be so grateful and stop always lecturing me and . . .' She trailed off.

'I think we should let Thomas have a go,' said Hinkypunk, languidly.

'And I,' said Adverse. 'If Thomas wants to do it, of course,' he added.

Angelica turned to Thomas. 'What do you think?'

'I'd like to, but only if Pinch and Patch can come too. And if Dad agrees,' he went on, seeing his father's anxious expression.

'You want to come?' said Roanna, surprised, turning to the twins. They nodded, in a rather surly way. 'That's really good! I'd really love you to come . . . And you're Thomas's best friends, after all.'

Pinch and Patch looked very embarassed indeed. Pinch mumbled, 'Nice of you,' and Patch whispered, 'I'd love to come, yes, if Mother doesn't mind.'

Thomas felt as if a great weight had been lifted off his shoulders.

'You can go, but so will I,' said Old Gal, firmly. 'I'll make up a potion and an ointment that will help to protect us in the sea for a time. And Pandora and Calliope are there too, so we'll be safe enough.'

'I know, dear lady, that you have the Horns of Pan now,' drawled Mr Tamblin, 'but you will remember, of course, that the sea has its own laws of magic, and that our own pishogue may not work as well there as here?'

The look Old Gal gave him then would have turned another person to stone. 'Thank you, Mr Tamblin,' she said coldly. 'But I am aware of it, and will act accordingly.' She turned to the children. 'Your own little bits of pishogue won't work there at all – no thinning, no long-stalking and no glamouring.' 'Thinning' was an invisibility spell, 'long-stalking' one that turned ordinary shoes into seven-league boots, and 'glamouring' was making something look like something it wasn't.

'I vote we equip them with a selection of goodies,' said Hinkypunk. 'You know how the Seafolk like presents. I'm happy to give a few of my most popular tricks.'

'And I a few suitable books,' said Monotype.

'And I think our Dr Fantasos can rustle up something good from his dream-lines,' said Mr Tamblin.

'Good idea,' said Angelica. 'In fact I'm sure we can get everyone in both Owlchurch and Aspire to contribute. Old Gal, how long do you think your protective mixtures will last?'

'A day and a night,' said Old Gal, 'but I'll take extras with me, in case we have to stay longer.'

'Fine. Now, you children can go to to Morph's Dreaming Emporium to pick up a batch of dream-boats. They're for messages, you see,' she said, when Thomas looked blank. 'They fold up small but they're very swift. You'll have to send us one when you arrive and then at regular four-hourly intervals so we know everything's going OK. If you miss a deadline, we'll set off at once to find you.'

'Very well,' said Old Gal.

Gareth spoke. 'Please, son, be careful. And don't be ashamed to send for help if you need it, will you?'

'I promise,' said Thomas, hugging his dad.

'I tell you another thing we must do before anyone goes,' said Mr Tamblin. He gestured with great disapproval at Roanna's clothes. 'And that's to make this poor girl more presentable. Now how about tootling over to Aspire with me, girl? I'm sure I can find some decent thing for you in Pandora's wardrobe. She keeps everything, even the things she used to wear as a girl. There'll be something in your size. Pandora won't mind.'

Thomas grinned to himself. He wasn't quite so sure the exquisite Pandora would love the idea of Roanna shuffling through her clothes!

ELEVEN

Thomas watched, fascinated, as Morph Onery, the hump-backed old dream-maker, carefully tweezered out a dozen or so of the frail little dream-boats from the big glass jar in which he kept them. The dream-boats were wispy, lacy and pale, like silhouettes cut out from paper doilies. Thomas wondered just how strong they really were. But he'd learned very quickly that nothing was as it seemed in the Hidden World, and that sometimes, the things that looked most solid were in fact not. And vice versa.

Morph dropped the dream-boats in a gossamer bag and handed them to Thomas. 'You take good care of them, mind,' he said. He looked sternly at Pinch who was crowding to look over Thomas's shoulder. 'And no monkey business either, Pinch Gull,' he added. 'No letting them out before the time they're meant to go.'

'Oh, no, sir!' protested Pinch, looking as if butter wouldn't melt in his mouth. 'The very idea, sir!'

'Hmm,' sniffed Morph. In a different tone, he added, 'Good luck, and take care, children. The sea is a wonderful place, but it can be treacherous and very dangerous. There's all kinds of people there. Don't take anything for granted.'

'We won't, Mr Onery, sir,' they said, solemnly, and took their leave.

They went around the village then collecting gifts to take to the Seafolk. From Hinkypunk, they got a firmly-tied brown paper parcel. 'It's a selection of my pretties,' the Trickster explained. 'Thought Seafolk kids might like 'em. There's a couple of Repeaters, and a Tail-puller, and three Mazers – I made those ones with Willy Wisp next door – and several Trippers, and three or four Ankle-biters. But beware – don't open the parcel yourselves, or the tricks will just scatter far and wide and cause havoc.'

From Monotype they got three books. Two of them were sharp and tough, snapping and clapping their pages with a warlike air. 'They're about sea battles,' said Monotype. 'I suggest giving one to the head of the Nerean Clan and one to the head of the Lochlans – but whatever you do, don't mention it to the other. They'll only find something else to fight about.' He opened one of the books at a page in the middle. There was an illustration of a couple of warships, firing on each other.

As Thomas looked, the illustration shook and wavered, and suddenly, there it all was in 3-D. He could smell the sea, see the sails billowing and the sea heaving, and hear the cannons roaring, the shouts of the sailors and the creaking of the ships. But it all stayed small, far away, like something you look at through the wrong end of a telescope. Then, as he watched, a mast came down on one of the ships, it tipped sideways, the cannons roared and tiny sailors jumped off the decks, the sea boiling all around them. And now Thomas could see forms moving under the surface of the sea, and people with sharp pointed faces and gleaming eyes snatching at sailors' legs, dragging them down . . . down . . . down . . .

'Oh, no!' he shouted, and shut the book with a snap. Monotype smiled faintly. 'Now then, here's the last book. This one is for the Proteans.'

It was small and dark blue, with a picture of a selkie on it and a curly title that said, in bright silver, 'The Hidden People of the Sea'.

'This is a very rare one,' said Monotype, stroking its soft cover. The book moved gently under his hand, and opened at an illustrated page, showing a merman in a fisherman's net, his beard all tangled up. Thomas heard his high, thin, wailing cry as the book snapped shut again.

'I got it in a junk shop in the Obvious World when I was out there one day,' said Monotype, happily. 'It's rather quaint – full of legends and rumours and half-truths, but it's quite fascinating. I added a grain or two of pishogue to it, to spice it up. I doubt the Proteans have anything like it on their shelves.'

There were more gifts – a box of gorgeous cakes, shaped like fish and decorated in coral colours, specially made to last in the sea, from Cumulus Zephyrus; some waterweed wine and sea-foam drops from Brigsein Nectar, the grocer; strings of tricksy fairy lights from Willy Wisp, the lighting man; from Adverse, a miniature model of Metallicus, complete with moans and groans; and lots more. From Aspire, there were also a good many wonderful things, from Miss Ambergris the baker's elegant sea-cloud cakes to one of Dr Fantasos's fabulous dream-projectors which unwound dreams like films inside sleepers' heads.

'Typical,' said Pinch, looking at the piles of gifts lying on a table in the Apple Tree. 'The stuff from Aspire looks twice as slick as ours.'

'Who cares?' said Patch, her eyes bright.

'Exactly, it's all amazing,' said Thomas. 'I wish we didn't have to give it all away.'

'Never mind,' said Angelica, who was writing down a tally of everything that was being sent. 'There's more of that where it comes from – and it might well play a big part in getting things sorted out. We have to make sure the presents are divided equally between the selkie clans, and to keep some for the Duchess of Oceanopolis, too – she's the ruler of the city. Ah, there you are, Old Gal,' she said, as the twins' mother came in with a small case in one hand. 'Everything ready?'

'Yes,' said Old Gal, pointing to the case. 'I've got enough doses for three days. Hopefully we'll be home long before that.'

'Hopefully,' said Angelica. Just then, a horn sounded outside – the hunting horn of Mr Tamblin's white car. 'Well, seems like they're set too.' She looked at Gareth, hovering a little anxiously nearby. 'Time for us to go.'

Thomas gave his father a quick, strong hug, then followed the others out. Mr Tamblin, Angelica and Old Gal got in the front seat next to the chauffeur Herne, while the children sat in the back seat. Roanna was already there, looking smart in a pair of soft pearl-grey stove-pipe trousers and a pale pink, shimmering shirt.

'Mr Tamblin said that Lady Pandora got this outfit from a travelling merman, but it shrank when she washed it and it's too small for her,' said Roanna, excitedly. 'It's woven from silkweed – the finest material there is in our realm! It'll be just as good as my second skin! I bet even the fine ladies in Oceanopolis don't have anything as smart as this!'

TWELVE

Shortly after, they took off, the big car suddenly sprouting graceful white wings, like those of giant seagulls. Under Herne's skilful hands, it rose straight up, then turned at the river and set off smoothly through the bright air.

'Look!' said Thomas, pointing. Past a wisp of flying cloud, he'd glimpsed, just for a moment in the distance, a beautiful golden house riding on a big fluffy cloud. In the next moment, it had vanished from sight, as another cloud cut it from view.

'Ariel country, you see,' said Patch. She pressed her nose against the glass. 'I've always wanted to go there. They say it's gorgeous.'

'Not as gorgeous as my country,' said Roanna. 'Oh!' she exclaimed as someone went zipping down past the window – a rather small someone with a handsome, laughing face, dressed in a pure white uniform with gold braid on it – and winged shoes!

'That's Captain Mercury,' said Mr Tamblin, turning around. 'He's the Ariels' messenger. In a hurry, isn't he? The Ariels are great lovers of music – harps, mostly. They'll be worried the curse will reach their lands too.'

'Could be quite a gathering down there,' said Angelica.

'Could be indeed,' drawled Mr Tamblin. 'Rather sorry I won't be there to see it, don't you know? Lucky you, Mrs Gull,' he said to Old Gal, 'but then, we couldn't have sent a better envoy, could we?'

Old Gal made a disbelieving sound in her throat. There was respect but not much sympathy between the twins' untidy mother and the elegant Aspirants.

The car sped smoothly on. Soon, they could see a shining silver line in the distance – the sea. A short time later, the car banked steeply down and came in to land on a deserted shelly beach.

Roanna had the door open even before they came to a complete stop. She fell out of the door, rolled on the sand, picked herself up, and looked around. 'It's over there!' she said, pointing. The spot didn't look any different from anywhere else on that beach, to Thomas. Roanna hobbled off, the others close on her heels.

As soon as she reached the spot, she began to dig. 'I've got them!' she said, triumphantly, brandishing a little drawstring bag. She opened it and pulled out the contents – two little dark silver caps, as close-fitting as bathing caps, made not of rubber, but of a soft, shiny material like sealskin. Shyly, she handed one to Thomas. 'That one's for you.' She put hers on, and touched it gently. She said, 'It's fine! I knew it would be! Wait a moment!' And she hobbled very fast to the edge of the sea, looked back at them, smiled and ran into the waves. She dived into the first wave, and disappeared. In an instant, she was up again, smiling and waving. 'Perfect! It's perfect! Oh, it's so good!' She rolled over in the wave and dived into the next one.

'That girl's going to get our nice seat all wet,' grumbled Mr Tamblin. 'Why don't we let her make her own way into the city?'

'I think we're going to need her as a guide,' said Old Gal, firmly.

Roanna ran out of the water. She shouted, 'Look! Look! Do you see him? There, on the horizon. Delfinus! He said he'd wait for me! Wait a moment!' She picked up a big shell. She put it to her ear, listened, held it up as if trying to find reception for a mobile phone, shook it, listened again, her face clearing. Then she put it to her mouth and spoke into it, words Thomas couldn't understand. But he'd heard those sounds before. She was talking dolphin language.

Roanna put the shell to her ear again and listened. She turned to them. 'He says all the clans have arrived in Oceanopolis for peace talks. And he'll take us into the city . . .'

'Time to swallow our medicine, then,' said Old Gal. 'Thomas, get that cap on too – Pinch and Patch and I won't need that sort of thing. I've mixed a spot of metamorph-herb into our own doses. It's no good for you, Thomas.' She was taking out bottles from her case as she spoke. 'There's also a jar of ointment – rub it all over your skin, or you'll shrivel up like a prune in no time.'

They drank the mixture – which tasted very nasty indeed – and rubbed the silvery ointment – which stung like mad for a moment – all over themselves. Thomas put the cap on. It rippled under his touch. He took his hand hastily away.

Strange things were happening to the twins. They still stayed basically Pinch and Patch size and form, but a long lacy ruff like a dorsal fin appeared on their backs, their feet lengthened and sprouted little silvery webs, and their hands too. Their untidy hair became sleek, shiny and close to their heads, and their eyes began to glow softly.

'You look rather like fin-folk,' said Mr

Tamblin, critically. 'Is that wise, Mrs G?'

Old Gal shrugged, and swallowed her own doses. But Roanna remarked, sharply, 'Anyone in their right mind can see they're not fin-folk. Those ones have shark fins, not pretty fish ones. Pinch and Patch look more like piscgars, really.'

'Oh, lord,' sighed Mr Tamblin. 'I just can't keep up with all those sea-tribes and clans — sounds all rather fishy to me!'

No one laughed.

They took off again, flying over the sea. All at once, Thomas felt a funny squirming in his belly. He said, 'I feel sick . . .'

'Don't worry,' said Old Gal, from the front seat, 'that's just the sea-mixture, beginning to take effect. It bubbles inside you and coats all your veins. That protects your insides from the sea, and also helps to keep the oxygen flowing. It's a bit like those diving-suits I've heard humans wear, except it works from the inside out. The ointment makes your skin waterproof, too.'

Thomas looked at his hands. They did seem different. It was as if someone had wrapped them in very fine clingfilm. He flexed them. They felt normal. He touched them. They felt slippery, and under the skin, he could suddenly see something spreading, like a moving sheet of water. His tummy bubbled and squirmed, not painfully this time, more like a tickle. Smiling, he looked down through the window over the wide expanse of deep blue sea, and all at once, he saw a broad silver back, leaping out of the water, and spied a friendly, laughing face. Delfinus, of course.

THIRTEEN

The water over the Golden Reef was clear as crystal. As the car hovered over it, Thomas could understand the name. The coral far below shone like pure gold.

Mr Tamblin was looking down a kind of telescope he'd popped up from the dashboard. 'Now then – let me see – yes, there, just where the reef ends, there's a good soft sandy landing place. That'll be perfect.' He put away the telescope. 'Mrs G, you'll have to pick up that sack of goodies and get into the back seat with the kids. As soon as the sea-beam is in place, the whole of the back will open up and you'll be whooshed straight down. Hold hands, tightly.'

'Good luck, and take care,' said Angelica.

Thomas gripped Old Gal's hand on one side and Patch's hand on the other. He swallowed.

'Right! Beam, on!' Mr Tamblin said, pushing a dashboard button. Through the window, Thomas saw a beam of silvery-white light appear outside. It was just like a ray of moonlight striking down from a cloud, cutting straight into the water below. Thomas's heart turned cartwheels. They were going down on *that*?

Mr Tamblin shouted, 'Ready – set – go!'

There was a sudden onrush of air, right under Thomas, and he fell, like a stone, down what seemed not like a beam now but like an enclosed slide, of the kind you get in public swimming pools in the Obvious World. Its sides were hard and clear as glass. He had lost Old Gal's and Patch's hands, and tumbled down, down, down, sliding faster and faster. He lost his balance and went head over heels, rolling like a ball.

In no time, he was at the bottom, tumbling with a thump on fine grey sand. Old Gal was already there, with the sack of presents, and Roanna.

'I'm just going up to get Delfinus,' said the selkie, and sprang up through the water like an arrow, heading to the surface.

In the next instant, Pinch and Patch whooshed down the slide, Pinch shrieking with glee. As soon as they were all on the sand, the slide's walls melted. The beam vanished. Thomas looked up through the clear water and saw, faintly, up in the distant sky, Mr Tamblin's car flying away, back towards the land. In a moment, it had disappeared.

Thomas looked around. They were in a sort of vast underwater meadow or park. In the distance, the Golden Reef loomed, like the ragged battlements of some huge castle rearing up to the sky. Here were a few scattered golden and pale pink and white coral polyps, like petrified trees, and tall dark seaweed waving in the undersea breeze, while underfoot the sand was dotted with patches of luminous green moss and weed. Tiny bright fish flitted like birds between the bony branches of the coral trees, and fat water snails and crabs grazed the bottom, like cattle. The air was a clear greeny-gold. Thomas took an experimental breath. It felt cool and pleasant.

'Look at me jump!' cried Pinch. 'I can go ever so high!'

Thomas tried it too. It was lovely. His feet left the ground and he floated. He pushed down again and touched the sand, then sprang up through the water like a released cork.

Not to be outdone, Patch said, 'I bet I can go right to the top!' But before she could get very far, she squealed and raced back down as a big silver body hurtled down towards them, Roanna riding on its back.

'Hoo-hoo!' boomed the dolphin. He nudged Thomas and made him fall over.

'And hello to you, too, Delfinus,' said

Thomas, picking himself up.

'Hoo-ta, hoo-fa,' the dolphin remarked, grinning.

Roanna slid down from his head and turned a lazy cartwheel. 'He says your friends look funny.'

'Funny yourself, big fish,' sniffed Pinch. The dolphin nudged him and opened his mouth wide. Pinch backed away in alarm and fell over Patch's feet. They both rolled on to the sand, then bobbed up again as the dolphin blew on them.

'Hoo-ta! Hoo-ta! Hoo-ta!' said the dolphin. No one needed a translation for that. It was plain he thought it was a very good joke and was laughing his head off.

'Oh, hilarious,' growled Pinch as they got their sea legs again. He shook a little fist in the direction of the dolphin. 'Try that again, big fat fish, and you'll see what's what . . .'

'Hoo-ta! Hoo-ta!' chortled the dolphin, blowing on him again.

Old Gal, who had been checking that everything they'd brought had survived the trip, looked up. She snapped, 'Roanna of the Protean Clan, I thought you said your friend Delfinus was very wise.'

'He is,' said Roanna, grinning. 'This is just his way of welcoming you all. It's the dolphin tradition.'

'Sure, sure,' muttered Pinch, sarcastically, keeping a wary eye on the dolphin, who smiled and dipped his head several times.

'Hoo-sa, Hoo-sa,' he boomed.

'Delfinus says he's sorry,' said Roanna, hugging him. 'He didn't mean to offend. He was just showing how pleased he was you were here. Now he's ready to take you into the city.'

'Hoo-la, hoo-la,' said the dolphin, dropping down low and swishing his tail.

Roanna said, 'He's telling you all to get on his back.'

'Catch me!' said Pinch, firmly, but he had no choice.

'Hang on!' whooped Roanna, as Delfinus took off speedy as a sports car, hurtling through the green air.

The sea-meadows soon gave way to the beginnings of settlement, with little houses dotted here and there, most on coral stilts, with roofs made of woven weed. They began to see a few people – some with tails – fish-tails and seahorse-tails – some with fins, some with legs (and some with several of those). Some swam about, some rode on fish, others on bicycle-like contraptions, with blades like skates instead of wheels, others still in frail little shell vehicles pulled by grumpy-looking crabs. Once, in the distance, they saw a big fat merman, with green hair and beard down to his golden, scaly waist, and a large pearl medallion. He was swaying high up on an embroidered saddle on a stately jellyfish, for all the world as if he were riding an elephant. 'He's a city nobleman,' explained Roanna. 'A member of the Duchess's family.'

A little later, they came to what looked like the entrance to a cave. There was a heavy barred grille set into it. The dolphin swam up to it and blew on the bars. 'Hoo-hoo, hoo-ma – hoo-Delf,' he proclaimed. At once, the grille creaked up to the roof of the cave, and the dolphin slipped into the darkness beyond, with everyone clinging to his back.

It was pitch black for a short while. Thomas couldn't even see his hand in front of his face. Just as he was beginning to feel a bit scared, the darkness lifted and they were back in the golden-green air again. Only this time they were in a big wide square, paved with multicoloured pebbles. All around them rose graceful buildings, some made of coral, some translucent like mother-of-pearl. Their roofs were tiled in amber, they were decorated with thousands of shells, and they had carved shutters made of pale driftwood. In front of each house there was a little mother-of-pearl tub, filled with waving little sea-flowers, in odd, attractive colours. In the centre of the square were large statues of a mermaid and a merman, riding on dolphins. Mermaids and mermen and creatures with fins on their backs like Pinch and Patch bustled about their business, swimming briskly around, gossiping to each other and hardly taking any notice of the newcomers.

'That's city people for you,' said Roanna. 'They're not curious about strangers. They like to think they've seen it all. Now if you'd come to our clan country, everyone would be interested in you.'

'They left the square and swished into the next street. This one was crowded with people, fish – who seemed to be used like horses or donkeys in the human world – and funny vehicles of the sort they'd seen outside of the city. The dolphin had to go along carefully, to avoid bumping into other traffic. Still, he was so big most people just got out of

the way. It was rather like riding a tank in a normal street, Thomas thought.

In this street, there was a long row of shops, with display windows made of thin, polished mother-of-pearl, and carved driftwood doors. One of them, Thomas noticed, had a row of silver oyster-shells above its door. The shells opened and shut, slowly, like blinking neon lights. Each time they opened, you could see the pearls inside them – grey, pink, yellow, white – glowing softly. It was enchanting. He pointed it out to Roanna.

'It's a jewellery shop,' she said. 'In fact, it's Pearlie's, the most famous jewellery shop in all the Seafolk lands. It has the prettiest things ever! Pretty posh and expensive too, I can tell you.'

'Could we have a quick look?' said Patch, shyly. Her eyes were like stars.

'What for . . .' Pinch began, but Delfinus came in closer, so that they hovered almost right up to the window. It was a gorgeous display: necklaces of red sea-gold and amber, coral rings and bracelets, and pearls in all kinds of settings – in rings, in earrings, as necklaces, as strings, as ropes, as brooches.

'I don't think the manager thinks much of our window-shopping,' said Old Gal, dryly, as a cross-looking merman's face appeared in the window and waved at them to go away. Delfinus grinned at him, but veered off anyway.

Thomas looked back to catch a last glimpse of the open-shut, open-shut oyster shells, and saw a customer coming out of the shop. She was a tall mermaid, with a beautiful, rather disdainful face, golden-skinned, raven-haired, with bright blue eyes the same colour as her elegant tail. She was followed by a whiskery old fish bent double under the weight of parcels on his back. For a beat of time, she stared at Thomas, and Thomas stared back. Her red lips opened, revealing white teeth as pointed as a fish's. She mouthed, softly, 'Come

here . . . come here . . . my sweet . . . come
here to me . . .'

Her hands reached out towards him, the
fingers long and slim, the nails curved like
talons. Her voice pulled at Thomas, calling to
something deep within him, fogging up all his
senses. Why, he thought, vaguely, I've heard
her voice before, she's kind and sweet and
beautiful, I must go to her this time, I must . . .

'Hey, what are you doing?' said Patch,
alarmed, grabbing at his arm as he began to
slide off the dolphin's back. Pinch grabbed at
the other arm. Old Gal steadied him back up,
and together they held him tight. But Roanna
had taken one look and urged Delfinus on. He
swam like the wind, and in an instant the street
with the shops had vanished behind them.

'Who ... who was that?' said Thomas.

'She was a Syren,' said Roaana. 'Most
mermaids are OK – though some are silly and
snobbish. But Syrens are different. They're
very dangerous. And they love humans – that

is they love their flesh and their blood and their bones.'

Thomas shivered. 'She was calling me,' he said.

'That's how they get their victims,' said Roanna. 'They often swim up to the surface of the ocean, calling to sailors, waiting for them to tumble off their decks into their arms – and *whoosh*! down they go. They drown them and then grind their bones to make their bread . . .'

'I'll give you some earplugs,' said Old Gal, with a reassuring look at Thomas. 'They can't do anything to you if you can't hear them.'

'Why do they . . . why do they let such people live here?' cried Thomas.

Roanna shrugged. 'The Syrens are a very ancient and wealthy race. They've always lived in the sea. They don't prey on Seafolk, so people tolerate them, though they're not liked. They keep themselves to themselves, mostly. And they guard against Uncouthers.'

'Oh – sort of like Peg Powler.'

'Yes. Sort of. The Syrens and the Uncouthers don't see eye to eye. But it still doesn't make 'em nice people. You want to keep away from them, Thomas.'

'I sure will,' said Thomas. He shuddered. 'I hope there's not too many of them about.'

'Oh no, not a huge lot,' said Roanna, jauntily. 'You don't often see them out and about. They mostly stay in their magnificent houses. They despise just about everyone else, you see, except for the Duchess and her family. That was the first time I'd seen one in ages. But then, I'm not often in the city.'

Patch's hand slipped into Thomas's clammy one. She whispered, 'Don't worry, Thomas. We'll look after you. We'll make sure those nasty Syrens stay well away.'

'We'll poke their eyes out,' said Pinch, in an undertone. 'Horrid old fishwives!'

Now the scene was changing. They'd come into a large area where there were big walled compounds, made of dark stone, draped with seaweed and decorated with large, unworked lumps of amber. No one was about, except for some sentries posted at the gates of the compounds. They were dressed in heavy, scaly armour, and their heads were hidden under big helmets. But their bare feet were flippered and hairy.

'This is the selkie quarter,' said Roanna, slipping off Delfinus's back. She pointed to a wall some distance away. 'That's my clan's compound. We'll swim there. Delfinus needs to get back up to the surface now.'

FOURTEEN

Inside the gates, there was a rather rough-and-ready sort of garden – a dark pebble path, a few stunted weeds and a sculpture made out of rusted iron, no doubt salvaged from a sunken ship. There were black steps leading up to a big square house, made of the same dark pebbles as the path but with a beautiful frieze over the door, made of white pearls. A big iron knocker in the shape of a seal was set into the door.

Roanna knocked. Very soon, the door opened, revealing a young selkie boy with spiky pale hair and sea-coloured eyes. He whistled.

'Roanna! Are you ever in trouble!' Then he

caught sight of everyone else. 'You've brought visitors! Who are they?'

'By Proteus, you can be rude,' said Roanna, impatiently pushing past him. 'Everyone, this is my cousin Telegon. Tel, meet Pinch and Patch Gull, and their mother Mrs Old Gal Gull. They come from up above, from Middler country.'

'How do you do?' said Telegon, hastily.

'And this is Thomas Trew. He's the Rymer I was telling you about.'

'Really?' said Telegon, staring at Thomas. 'I've never seen a Rymer before. You look different to what I thought.'

'What did you expect?' said Roanna, before Thomas could get a word in. 'Rymers are just human beings.'

'We don't see many of those either,' said Telegon. 'Except dead ones,' he added, matter-of-factly.

'OK, that will do,' said Old Gal, sharply. 'If you don't mind, young Telegon, we've got work to do. And we must get on to it at once.'

'The curse, you mean?' Telegon breathed. 'They're all having a big pow-wow about it in the meeting-room.'

'Who?' said Roanna.

'All of our lot, and the Nereans too. I'll take you in.' Telegon picked up the sack of presents. His eyes shone. 'Hey, this is heavy! Can't wait to see what you brought!'

He looked rather lively and cheerful for someone under a curse, thought Thomas, puzzled. But Roanna solved that one by saying, 'Tel was born with tin ears. He's never liked music much. Sad, for a selkie, isn't it? I reckon it's one of our human ancestors coming out in him.'

'Oh you're always reckoning something,' said Telegon, crossly. 'You're a caution, you are, that's what Grandmother says.' They set off down the hallway.

'Is Grandmother really angry?' said Roanna.

'She said you'd be grounded for a year. At

least,' said Telegon. He pushed open a door at the end of the hall. 'This way.'

They were in one of the most unexpected rooms Thomas had ever seen. Actually, it was more like a passageway – a sort of huge glass-walled bubble beyond which he could see a kind of sea-garden, very different to the one they'd seen earlier. Seaweed bushes hung with coloured lights swayed in the sea air. Glass baubles in the shapes of seals and whales and dolphins and fish tinkled from coral branches. In the very middle stood a bronze statue of an old man wearing a toga and a crown of seaweed. Around his neck was wreathed a rope of shining pearls. At his feet were baskets of sea-flowers. 'Our revered ancestor, Proteus,' said Telegon, proudly. 'Isn't he grand and dignified?'

'He surely is,' said Old Gal. She was casting a shrewd look around. 'Do you know, I think this is a good place to send a dream-boat from. Plenty of light. Thomas, hand me the bag.

Now watch carefully, children, in case you need to do it yourselves.'

She reached into the bag and gently took out a dream-boat. It looked frail, almost faded, in her hand. She put it gently against the glass, where it stuck at once. Its outline grew stronger, more filled in. The sail seemed to move, just a little. Old Gal came close to it, and blew gently on it. She whispered, 'Swift, little boat, swift, and say this: Safely here, will send more very soon, cheers, Old Gal.' She paused and blew on the dream-boat again, harder this time. At once, the sail bellied out, the hull jerked, the glass under it wavered and rippled, then the dream-boat passed through it, and straight out into the sea-garden. For an instant they could see it floating lightly on the currents, then the frail sail bellied again and it shot straight as an arrow to the surface and disappeared.

'Oh, that was so beautiful,' breathed Telegon, speaking for them all. 'I've never seen such beautiful pishogue, not ever . . .'

'I daresay you've got just as good here,' said Old Gal, dryly.

Telegon shook his head. 'Oh, with us it's just about music and stuff,' he said, 'nothing like as useful as that dream-boat. I wish I could make things like that . . .'

'Well, you should get apprenticed to a dream-maker, then,' said Old Gal, laughing. 'Now then, we'd better get on, eh?'

The meeting-room was large, noisy, very crowded and rather stuffy. Selkies of all ages sat around a vast driftwood table, arguing. At first, no one noticed Thomas and his friends – the selkies were too busy shouting. But soon, the noise died down and the clans turned to look at the strangers.

Telegon proclaimed, 'Clan Protean, Clan Nerean, I announce to you the coming of welcome guests – the Gulls from Middler country, and Thomas Trew, the Rymer. They were brought here by a daughter of Clan Protean, Roanna, who begs your leave to bring them into our midst.'

It was a daunting feeling, staring into all those eyes. Thomas could feel them searching his face, trying to see into his head. There was no way of telling what the selkies were feeling. Their faces were set, impassive. They were very still. Their second skins shining in the soft light and sleek hair close to their heads made them look rather like metal statues themselves.

Then one of the selkies got up. She was small, bent, but with bright eyes and bright hair that reminded Thomas instantly of Roanna. In a strong, sweet voice, she said, 'On behalf of Clan Protean, I, Idothea of the Protean Clan, welcome the Middlers and the Rymer to our house. I thank my granddaughter Roanna for bringing such welcome guests' – here Roanna couldn't stop herself from sticking out her tongue at Telegon – 'but I ask her also,' went on Roanna's grandmother in a suddenly stern tone, 'to come and see me afterwards.'

'Yes, Grandmother,' said Roanna, meek for the first time.

Another selkie got up. It was a man this time, a tall, fierce-faced old selkie with an impressive pair of whiskers and a nearly bald head. He growled, 'And I, Morgan of the Nerean Clan, do wish to add our welcome to that of the Clan Protean. We are most grateful for your interest and your efforts in helping us track down the perpetrator of this dastardly crime. Hail, and welcome, to the Middlers and the Rymer!'

'Hail and welcome!' came the cry from all around the room, as selkies old and young, big and small, rose to their feet and cheered. Thomas and the Gulls bowed and smiled and smiled and bowed, and thanked everyone, and when the noise had died down, Old Gal took out the presents from the sacks. They were all a great hit, and the chieftains said a great many flowery words of thanks.

Then Old Gal said a few words herself – but her usual plain ones – about how they were glad to be here, but they had a job of work to do, and would need to ask a lot of questions. Idothea and Morgan assured her that all their clansmen and clanswomen would be happy to answer anything, but that everyone knew it was the Lochlans behind it all. Old Gal nodded, and said nothing more, but Thomas could see she wouldn't let it rest there.

'Now, then, tonight we will have a feast in your honour,' said Idothea, grandly. 'I'll wager you'll never have tasted such a feast – our head cook Clytie is the best chef in all the Seafolk lands.'

'Except ours,' smiled Morgan. 'Our Myrrie won the Pan-Ocean Gold Cup last year, remember.'

'Hmph! Well, Clytie'll win this year. Her Proteus Pudding will see to that!'

'It is very nice, that I'll admit,' said Morgan,

eyes gleaming, 'but I'm sure Myrrie could make something just as good.'

'Shall we make a wager, dear sir?' said Idothea, smiling a little thinly now.

'At your service, dear lady,' beamed Morgan.

'We'll decide the terms later, Lord Morgan. For now, I think our guests are in need of rest and refreshment. May I offer you our guest quarters?'

'Some of them could stay with us,' suggested Morgan. 'Perhaps the ladies could go to you and the gentlemen to us?'

Patch looked alarmed. 'I want to stay with my brother and Thomas,' she whispered.

'We'll take it in turns, then, Morgan,' said Idothea. 'Tonight, we'll have the honour. Tomorrow night, it will be yours. Agreed?'

'Agreed,' said the old selkie.

Old Gal coughed. 'If you don't mind,' she said, 'I need to compare notes with Calliope and Pandora, and the sooner the better. Are they staying here?'

'Oh no,' said Idothea. 'They're being put up by the Duchess.'

'Well, then, I will go there,' said Old Gal, firmly. 'I am in no need of rest.'

'I think they're at the Lochlans' compound right now, asking questions,' said Morgan.

'Then I'll just take myself over there,' said Old Gal, firmly, forestalling any objections.

'Can we come with you, Mother?' said Pinch.

'No,' said Old Gal. 'It won't be interesting anyway. Just going over old ground. And I'll be back soon. Now then, if someone could please direct me to the Lochlan compound, I'll be off straight away.'

FIFTEEN

'You know what?' said Thomas. 'I've been thinking.'

'Careful,' said Pinch. 'You might burst that big hero's brain of yours. And that would really upset Roanna!'

'Oh, ha, ha,' said Thomas. 'No – what I've been thinking is something weird's going on.'

It was night, and the twins and Thomas had gone to bed in the big, green-lit upstairs room they'd been given. The beds were high and carved, and next to them were round windows that gave on to the sea outside. Thomas could see fish swimming past.

Downstairs, the selkie party was still going on. The children could hear faint, muffled noises coming from it.

Pinch raised an eyebrow. 'Really! Tell us something we don't know!'

'Oh, shut up,' said Patch, crossly. 'Let Thomas explain.'

'I mean – well, you heard what your mother said, when she came back from the Lochlan compound, that the Lochlans are sure the whole thing's a plot against them. But she also said they didn't seem at all affected by the curse. They can sing and play just as well as ever. And yet the curse is supposed to just go wild really quickly. It's supposed to be uncontrollable…'

'The Proteans have definitely got it,' said Patch. 'You saw how they covered up their ears when Mother played that tune on Calliope's flute? And don't you dare say what I think you're about to say,' she added, glaring at her brother. 'Mother can't play as well as Calliope, but she's not bad.'

'Well, that's true – I mean, that the music

seemed to hurt their ears,' said Thomas, hastily, 'but you see, what's odd too is that *noise* doesn't seem to please them either. Did you notice, when the servant dropped that metal plate, everyone winced and shouted at him?'

Pinch stared at him. 'So what? It was a horrid noise.'

'I just thought – it's funny – music sounds like noise to them, but noise doesn't sound like music, it still sounds like noise.'

'But why shouldn't it?' said Pinch, after a little silence. 'I don't get it.'

'Well, it just got me thinking. How did this curse actually work? So I asked Telegon if he'd covered his ears when the music played, and he said no, what was the point? I then asked him about the clattering plate, and he said it was a horrid noise. I asked him if it sounded like music to him – and he stared at me and said of course not, it's just a noise, isn't it? Then I asked him about the music Old Gal had played – and do you know what he said?'

'No,' said the twins together, agog.

'He said to him it was just the same as usual, one note after another. You remember how Roanna said he had a tin ear, which was unusual in a selkie? Music bores him, he said. He didn't see the point of it. And that hadn't changed.'

Patch said, slowly, 'But maybe he's always heard music as if it was noise?'

Thomas shook his head. 'I asked him that. He says he can tell the difference easily. And that hasn't changed – despite the curse.'

'But maybe the curse doesn't affect him, because he's got a tin ear,' said Pinch.

'No. You heard them talking about how the curse works, didn't you? It affects *all* selkies – or should. It's like a poison that attacks selkie blood. Then I thought, *why* is Telegon immune?'

'Maybe there's others who are, too,' said Patch. 'People you haven't asked.'

'Maybe,' said Thomas. 'I did ask quite a lot of

them, though. I also watched to see how the Nereans reacted to the music. Did you?'

'Can't say I did,' said Pinch.

'No, you were too busy hoeing into that amber-cream cake,' said Patch.

'Well, it was better than that horrid Proteus Pudding they think is so great,' said Pinch. 'Pooh! I reckon it smelled bad. Maybe the curse has taken away their sense of smell, too. Did you have any, Thomas?'

Thomas said, impatiently, 'No. Didn't like the look of it. Well, did you notice what the Nereans did, Patch, when they heard the music?'

'I didn't notice then,' said Patch, honestly, 'but I'm trying to think back now – and I think that some of them seemed to like it and others didn't.'

'Exactly – that's what I saw, too. I reckon some of them have the curse and others don't. You see – it's all quite strange. Why have only some people got it and not others? Is this how the curse works normally?'

'How would we know?' said Pinch.

'We'll have to try and find out tomorrow,' said Thomas.

'Please don't let's tell the adults about your idea,' said Patch. 'Not yet, anyway. Let's try and work this out on our own.'

'OK. We're safe here, I suppose,' said Thomas. 'Unless we get the curse too.'

'Doesn't seem likely to me,' said Patch. 'I heard that music perfectly well. I reckon the curse is a lot weaker than they said it was.'

Pinch gave an exclamation. 'I've just had a thought!'

'Careful, now,' said Thomas, earning himself a glare.

'I've just had a thought,' went on Pinch, doggedly. 'Maybe the Proteans are just making a big deal of it all. Maybe they're not really cursed, they just *think* they are. I mean, they say the Lochlans threatened to curse them after the Proteans pinched that song . . .'

'The Proteans deny they did,' Thomas

reminded him.

'Yes, but it doesn't mean it isn't true. Maybe the Proteans just feel guilty, and then they hear the Lochlans threaten to curse them and they're sure it's true . . .'

'I can't believe that,' said Thomas. 'No one could put on an act like that. You saw how they reacted to the music. That was genuine. And if some of the Nereans too are coming down with it, that proves it's real. Besides, you saw the risks Roanna took. She wouldn't do that for nothing.'

'Maybe she *thought* it was real,' said Pinch.

'It *is* real!' said Thomas, crossly. 'Everyone else here seems to think it is, and I'm sure Seafolk would know more about a water-curse than you, right?'

'OK, OK,' said Pinch, quickly. 'I agree, your precious Proteans aren't putting it on. But where does that leave us?'

'With more time than we thought,' said Thomas. 'I think Patch is right. This is a much weaker curse than they said.' He yawned. 'Let's talk about it all tomorrow and work out what to do.'

'And no adults,' said Pinch, firmly.

'Sure. But Roanna and Telegon could help quite a lot.'

'Do they *have* to tag along?' said Patch.

'They're selkies. They know things we don't,' said Thomas. 'And you shouldn't be jealous,' he added, under his breath, but the twins didn't hear him. They were too busy trying to get their dorsal fins to fold flat so they could lie down comfortably. Thomas was fast asleep before they finally managed it.

SIXTEEN

Thomas woke suddenly in the middle of the night. His tummy felt empty. He lay there for a little while, trying to ignore the pangs of hunger. Despite Idothea's boast about the Protean cook, nothing much at the banquet had taken Thomas's fancy. Everything was all so fishy or seaweedy or odd. Some things looked downright disgusting, like a plate full of fish heads whose boiled eyes and gaping jaws stared at Thomas. And that Proteus Pudding had smelled like something that had died in stagnant water. Yuck! He had picked at a few things, like fish in a white sauce or sea-greens with mustard, and he'd had a small slice of that amber-cream cake, which had tasted OK though not exactly delicious, with a fishy aftertaste even there. Trouble was, he was used to tasty Middler cooking, and Cumulus Zephyrus's heavenly cakes and pastries.

He could just see one of them in his mind's eye now – all puffed and golden and singing with cream. His mouth watered. His tummy rumbled. Oh dear! He must go and get something to eat, or he'd be sick. Maybe there was something plain – some biscuits, or bread – that he could scrounge for in the kitchen.

He got up and put on his shoes and a dressing-gown borrowed, like his pyjamas, from selkie wardrobes. It was too big for him, and he had to tie the cord twice around his waist. But it was warm, and that was good, for out of bed, the big room felt rather cold. He looked at Pinch and Patch. They were fast asleep. For a moment, he thought of waking them. Pinch had eaten heaps at dinner, but he was always ready to eat more. And both twins would enjoy a raid down in the kitchen. But no – they looked so peaceful. He didn't want to disturb them.

He took the sea-light that had been left on a chair for them and lit it. Sea-lights are phosphorescent plants which Seafolk grow in tall, closed glass pots. A little knob on the side of the pot controls the plant, which when unlit looks just like a pale sort of weed but when lit glows with a steady, if rather ghostly, light. By its light Thomas tiptoed across the room and out of the door. He looked down the corridor. There was nobody around. The sound downstairs had stopped too. The selkies must finally have gone to bed.

Thomas stepped out into the corridor, closing the door behind him. He hurried down the passageway to the stairs. His room was on the second floor. On the first floor were more bedrooms, and on the ground floor meeting-rooms and the big banquet-hall. Thomas knew the kitchen was in the basement, directly

141

under the banquet-hall, as some of the dishes had come up in a lift thing from down there. He scuttled down the first set of stairs. He checked, suddenly. He'd heard a noise. But it was only the sound of someone snoring, very loudly, behind one of the closed doors. He went down the next set of stairs. All was dark and silent. Passing the banquet-hall, he peeked in. The servants must have been busy. The room, which had been a shambles when Thomas last saw it, had been cleaned and tidied for the morning. Plates were already set out for breakfast.

The basement stairs were at the opposite end to the banquet-hall. They were rather dark, steep and twisty, and smelled strongly of the sea. The air got thicker here, too, and Thomas felt almost as though he was swimming down. But he still wore the selkie cap, so he was OK going down into the watery darkness.

The kitchen was a relief. It was filled with soft green-gold light. Pots and pans gleamed.

But there was nothing to eat there, except for bunches of dried sea-herbs and a large jar of tiny shiny dried fish. Selkies ate these like sweets. They didn't appeal to Thomas at all.

Then he found the pantry. Wow! It was stocked to the rafters with food. More sea-herbs in bunches, and fish-ham, wrapped in seaweed bags, and smoked oysters and mussels and fish. Tall sacks of seaweed flour and jars of seaweed jam. Jellyfish soup in cans and sea-sugar in sachets. And yes – in a big tin, a pile of large pale biscuits. Thomas sniffed them – hmm, not too fishy. They would have to do. Thomas grabbed a generous handful, put them in his dressing-gown pocket, and shoved a couple more biscuits into his mouth. They weren't too bad – rather salty, but quite tasty. He munched, and swallowed. He was about to take another one, when suddenly, he heard voices. Someone was coming into the kitchen!

Thomas turned off the lamp, put the tin carefully back on the shelf, and hid behind the sacks of flour. At first, he couldn't hear what the voices were saying. They were muffled by the closed door. But then he heard it opening. He pressed back into the shadows behind the sacks, hoping it wasn't flour they were after.

'Are you quite sure nobody saw you coming in?' said a voice. Thomas recognised it at once. It was Clytie, the Proteans' head chef. Big, round and gruff, she had been brought out from the kitchen to take everyone's congratulations, at dinner.

'Oh no! I slipped in silent as a ghost, quiet as a mist, madam. But I sensed you needed me to come. It doesn't do, dear madam, to run out of your best ingredients – especially when you have visitors, and at trying times like this,' said another voice. The hair rose on the back of Thomas's neck. There was something about the soft, sly tones of that voice, despite its total politeness, that made him feel very uneasy indeed. He held his breath.

'You're right. I did need more,' said Clytie.

'But I was going to get a message to you tomorrow morning.'

'Tomorrow morning you would not find me,' said the sly voice. 'I am going on a journey.'

'Oh, indeed?' said Clytie distractedly. 'Well, then it was good of you to come. Everybody would so have missed it if it hadn't appeared on the tables tomorrow.'

'You see, I was right, wasn't I?' said the sly voice. 'Your dish pleases all. And your reputation grows by the day.' Thomas badly wanted to see who it belonged to, but at the same time he was too scared to try and look. He couldn't even tell if it was male or female. 'I guarantee that next Gold Cup will be yours, nothing surer. The fame of your dish will spread everywhere. Have you tasted Clytie's Proteus Pudding, they'll say? Only Clytie can make it like Proteus himself – praise his dear memory – used to serve it at his table, long long ago when all the worlds were young...'

'You really think so?' Clytie's voice was

145

dreamy. 'You really think they'll talk about me like that?'

'Indeed I don't merely *think*, madam, I *know*. You will be famous throughout the seven seas, in this world and even the Obvious World.'

'I hope you're right. Now, is this batch exactly like the others?'

'Oh yes, my dear lady. Nothing but the best for you. A paste of the finest pearls, ground up in the finest fish-oil, finished with just a dash of dream-dust, and then carefully filtered through a—'

'Spare me the sales talk,' said Clytie, back to being gruff. 'I'm already sold on it. I suppose next you'll tell me the price has gone up.'

'Oh, I'm afraid, my dear lady, that it has, just a little. Just a little . . .'

'It goes up every time,' snapped Clytie.

'It's rare, madam. All such rare ingredients! And it is not easy to get them – the hardships I've had to go through, the—'

'Very well,' said Clytie. 'I'll pay a little extra.

The Nereans liked it too and they'll be coming over again tomorrow. But don't think you can do this all the time, or—'

'Or what, dear lady?' hissed the sly voice, becoming suddenly menacing. 'Or else you'll tell someone? But then you'd have to tell them you've been dealing with outlaws and outcasts, for isn't that what they call us?'

'Stop it,' said Clytie, and all at once she sounded frightened.

The creature laughed, a horrible, gurgling sound. 'I rather think – yes – I rather think I'd better raise that price again. Twice over. After all, I had to go to a lot of trouble this time. And there's a few too many busybodies around for my liking . . .'

'And for mine,' said Clytie, 'which is why I didn't want you coming here.'

'Oh, dear lady, perhaps you want to end our arrangement?' Thomas heard a shuffling step moving away from the pantry, towards the door. 'I'll take my little bag of goodies away, shall I? And then you'll feel safe again.'

'No, no, I didn't mean that.' Clytie sounded desperate. 'Everyone loves it, it's one of the few things makes them happy right now, what with this terrible curse . . .'

'Ah, yes, the terrible curse,' said the sly voice. 'Madam, perhaps I could help you there too.'

'You are a fool. Creatures such as you have no means of undoing the curse. You are the dregs of the sea. And I've heard quite enough from you. Take your money.' Thomas heard the clink of coins. 'Now give the pearl-paste to me. I'll put it away, right now.'

Thomas heard her rattling around on the shelves. He crouched down in a ball, trying to will himself into a stony stillness.

'Now you must go. Leave by the cellar. I'll unlock the gate for you. And you must not come here again, under any circumstances,' Clytie added, and now her voice was fierce. 'You must wait till I come to you, do you understand?'

'Oh, yes, my lady,' whined the soft voice. 'I understand.'

The pantry door slammed shut. Footsteps moved rapidly across the kitchen, then that door slammed too. Thomas was left alone.

SEVENTEEN

Taking his lamp, but not lighting it, Thomas slipped out of the pantry and carefully opened the kitchen door. He looked out into the passageway beyond. He could not see them, but he could hear their footsteps receding in the opposite direction, towards the cellar steps. Thomas took a deep breath, then set off after them.

They'd left the cellar door ajar. Thomas could see a faint light down there, bobbing about. He could hear locks clicking open, and the grind and squeak of a heavy gate. He heard Clytie's voice, murmuring something. The sea-stink was very strong now, but Thomas thought, I have to follow that creature, I have to know who it is, and why it thinks it can help with the curse . . . But how would he get out if the gate was locked again? He'd have to stop Clytie from doing so.

An idea leaped into his head. He waited till he heard Clytie begin to close the gate again, then he threw his lamp as hard as he could, down the corridor through which he'd just come, and dived behind the door. The glass shattered on the hard floor of the passageway and the sea-light ball popped out and let out a shriek. Clytie dropped her keys and ran up the cellar steps and into the dark passageway, crying, 'Who's there? Who's there?'

Thomas slipped out from behind the door without her seeing him, and down the cellar steps. He reached the gate. It was not quite closed. He squeezed through the small opening and found himself in a narrow alleyway. At the end of it, he could see a scuttling, hurrying dark shape. Thomas didn't hesitate this time. He set off in pursuit.

The alley gave out on to another alley, and into another. The air grew thicker, darker; the waterweed waved over Thomas's head. But with the selkie cap on his head, he could breathe more or less easily though he couldn't move as fast as he'd have liked. But he still managed to keep the figure in view. His eyes had adjusted to the watery darkness a little, and he could see that the creature had a triangular dark fin on its back, poking out of its hooded cloak.

Down one more alley, then the creature took a right turn and came out into a rather wider street. It was lined with high blank walls, like those in the selkie quarter. The creature hurried down the street, till it came to a door set into one of the walls. Thomas hung back in the shadows, watching. The creature rapped twice, said, 'Hail to the Kin,' the door opened, and he disappeared inside.

I've gone too far to turn back now, thought Thomas. He went swiftly to the door, rapped twice, said, 'Hail to the Kin,' in as sly and soft a voice as he could manage. The door opened, and he stepped through. It slammed shut behind him with a final sort of sound.

He was alone in a square pebbled courtyard, set in front of a large white house. The sea-air here was clearer, lighter, easier to breathe. In the middle of the courtyard was a weird sort of garden, whose beds had borders made of shining white sticks. In the beds stood strange lopsided statues which ended at the waist. It took Thomas a little time to realise they were the figureheads of ships – and that the 'sticks' were in fact bleached bones – most likely human bones. His heart began to pound. What was this place? He went back to the door. It was shut fast. He looked up at the wall. It loomed high and sheer and unfriendly. There was no way he could climb it.

Well, there's nothing for it, thought Thomas. I have to go to the front door of that house, knock and say to whoever answers that I'm the Rymer and that I've come to ask them questions. After all, Rymers have a special standing everywhere in the Hidden World, and even Uncouthers think twice about hurting them. And these people aren't Uncouthers. This isn't even Mirkengrim. It's Oceanopolis, after all. And that's a civilised place. No one would hurt a Rymer here . . .

Telling himself these things, he marched to the house. He climbed up the front steps and knocked on the door. Once, twice, three times. He heard footsteps approaching. The door opened, revealing a magnificent glittering marble hall beyond, filled with beautiful blue-gold light – and a bent old woman on the doorstep.

She didn't match that beautiful hall. She was badly-dressed, with a triangular fin on her back, purple and ragged this time. Apart from the fin, she looked like a toad, with a loose, jowly green-yellow face and bulging, rather bloodshot eyes. Thin, greenish-grey hair was plastered on her scalp and her bare scaly feet rasped on the marble of the floor. She peered short-sightedly at Thomas. 'Who is the stranger who calls on the Kin at this time of night?'

'I am the Rymer,' said Thomas, carefully.

'The Rymer, eh?' cackled the old woman. 'The mistress'll be expecting you, then.'

'What do you mean?' cried Thomas.

An expression of sly glee flitted across the old woman's ugly face. 'She knew you'd end up here, one of these days. Well, well, sooner than she thought, I say. Well, come along, Rymer.'

'I don't want . . .' Thomas gabbled, seized by panic, then recovered and said, 'You know that a Rymer has safe passage here and all the lands of . . .'

'Of course, of course,' said the little old woman. She shuffled close to Thomas and laid a bony hand on his arm. 'Hmmm. Rymer not too fat, say I.' She pinched Thomas's skin between finger and forefinger.

He yelped, and jumped away from her.

'Leave me alone, you horrible old hag!'

'Ha ha ha!' chortled the old woman. 'Rymer is scared, yes? Me, I can smell fear . . . I can smell it paces away . . . long, long away . . . But you need not fear, Rymer. We know old traditions. We keep to them. Rymer – out of bounds for us. We do not kill or eat your sort. You do not need to fear. We want to help you. My mistress – she knows much about the curse. One of her family, she helped that old Rymer, long ago.' Her mouth split into a rather scary grin, showing lots of razor-sharp teeth, planted close together. 'Ha, they did not tell you that, did they, those foolish selkies! Ashamed of it, they are, though the Kin are older and greater than they! Come, Rymer. You come and talk to mistress. She will tell you what to do – then you go and tell everyone, be a hero – go home. What could be simpler?'

Her voice had changed, it had become sweet, soft, caressing, almost as though it was someone else's voice, coming from her mouth. 'Come, come, my pretty, my dear,' the old woman crooned, and Thomas could feel his limbs moving of their own accord, and his head filling up with fog. 'Come, my dear, follow my servant, and let me tell you all . . .' And this time Thomas followed, in a dream, through the glittering marble hall and into a wide corridor whose walls were painted with vivid pictures of shipwrecks and storms at sea.

They came to a door in the corridor. The old woman knocked. Once, twice. The sweet voice called, from beyond the door, 'Come in, come in, my sweet, my pretty . . .'

The old woman opened the door, and Thomas stepped through, to find himself in a beautiful pale blue and green room, whose ceiling was painted with stars that seemed to twinkle with gentle silver light. One wall of the room was made entirely of glass, and behind it was the sea, and bright fish darting like living jewels among green plants. A large pool, tiled with blue and green mosaics and filled with crystal-clear water, was set into the middle of the marble floor. Floating in the pool was a beautiful creature, raven-haired, blue-eyed, golden-skinned. She wore a blue bodice, pale green flowers twined into her hair, pearls around her neck and wrists and on her fingers, and her graceful fish-tail was of the same bright blue as her eyes.

'My dear Rymer, my pretty,' she said, in her soft voice, 'how glad I am to meet you properly at last! My name is Cirsea, and I've been waiting for you . . .'

'You're a Syren,' said Thomas, the fog clouding his brain but not quite blotting out everything. 'I saw you this afternoon, near Pearlie's.'

'We prefer to be called the Kin,' said the Syren, gently. 'Yes, I tried to call you to me this afternoon, but your friends stopped you.

158

Jealous, I think, that you are a Rymer, and so much more important than they are . . .'

'They said you would hurt me,' said Thomas, dazedly, and already it seemed to him like an impossible idea, that such a beautiful creature could ever hurt anyone. Cirsea gave a merry, tinkling little laugh.

'They are jealous and rude, dear Rymer – sweet Thomas,' she said, and so fogged was Thomas now that he didn't even realise she had called him by his proper name. 'As if I would ever hurt a Rymer – besides, it's not allowed. You're no ordinary human. And I'm rich and comfortable here, the greatest of the Kin. Do you really think I want to be banished to Mirkengrim? Do you think I want to spoil my life just for a sweet crunch of human bone?' Her teeth flashed as she spoke – such sharp, sharp white teeth – but Thomas was too dazed to notice. 'No, Thomas dearest, I want to help you. Come, sit by me, and I will tell you what it is you need to do to undo the selkie's curse.'

And in a dream, Thomas did just as he was told.

EIGHTEEN

'You see,' said the Syren, smiling up at Thomas, 'long ago, a selkie fell in love with one of the Kin. Though they should have been honoured – for we are the most ancient of the sea-races, apart from our servants the fin-folk – his family forbade the match. So in a fit of rage he created the Curse of Cacophony. It went like wildfire through all the selkie clans, causing death and destruction wherever it went.'

'Oh, that was the wicked selkie I heard about,' said Thomas.

'They called him wicked, just because he loved one of us,' said Cirsea, sorrowfully. 'He was banished, and very soon died. And the

Kinswoman who had been his love grew sad at what had happened. She resolved to help the selkies, though they turned from her in disgust. We Kin have deep knowledge, Thomas, and so soon she learned that the curse must be ended by another betwixt and between creature, similar to selkies but different – a creature of both human and Hidden blood. She found that such a creature existed, and that its name was Thomas – Thomas the Rymer, or True Tom. So she contrived to have a message sent to him, and he came to the realm of the sea . . .'

'Like me,' said Thomas, wonderingly.

'That's right, dearest. Exactly like you,' she crooned, and laid her golden hand on his own hand, making a weird shiver ripple through him. 'Exactly like you, except he was older – a good deal older. You are even stronger than he was, because your gifts have shown so young. You see, I have heard such tales of you – how brave you are, how clever, how good at solving puzzles and mysteries and understanding things. I never heard of such a gifted Rymer as you before. And that's why I knew I must ask your help.'

'Really?' said Thomas, happily.

'Really,' said the Syren. 'Now, you see,' she went on, 'what you must understand is this – even before the Rymer came, the Kinswoman had realised that just as music is the food of life for selkies, so noise is their poison.'

'I've heard that before,' said Thomas, dreamily. 'But I don't remember where.'

'It doesn't matter,' said Cirsea, and her eyes glowed with a red light then, but Thomas didn't notice. 'You see, she knew that poison must be countered with antidote. And so she had found a mixture that was not quite antidote but that retarded the effects of the curse – a mixture of pearls ground in the finest fish-oil, laced with dream-dust, and filtered in sand from the deepest part of the ocean . . .'

'Oh,' said Thomas, staring, as the words

164

pierced through the pleasant fog in his mind. 'Then that means . . .'

'Oh yes, Thomas, dear, that means it's happening just the same again. Wait a moment. You'll see.' She clapped her hands, once, twice, three times. The door opened, and a sly voice said, 'You called, my lady?'

Thomas turned. It was the creature he'd followed from the Proteans' house. Now he could see its face properly. It was a very ugly one, with smooth grey skin and little red eyes and a lipless mouth, like a shark's.

'Yes, Aikelos,' said Cirsea. 'Come in. This is my servant, Aikelos,' she said to Thomas.

The creature shot a sly glance at him, then at its mistress, who said, smoothly, 'Tell Thomas what we've been doing, Aikelos, to protect those ungrateful selkies.'

'Oh, yes, mistress,' said the creature, humbly. 'I will tell Rymer, I will. You see, young master, we've been shielding them from the worst of the curse this time too, and they don't even know it. My lady Cirsea had the recipe for the paste made by her ancestor, but we couldn't just tell them about it. You see, they have an unjust horror of the Kin – not knowing how my lady's ancestor helped the Rymer, or likely, not wanting to know.'

'The selkies have many qualities,' said Cirsea, watching Thomas, a gentle smile on her face, 'but I'm afraid clear thinking is not one of them. They are wild and hasty and impatient and proud and quarrelsome. It irks them to think they could be helped by strangers, and most especially, the Kin . . .'

'That's so unfair,' cried Thomas, 'when it was the Kin who helped them last time!'

'I know,' said the Syren, and bright tears like diamonds glittered in her eyes. 'But that is the way of the world, dear Thomas. I knew I could not approach them directly. So I set up my servant Aikelos with a stall in the midnight markets – they are held once every moon here – because I knew Clytie, the Proteans' cook, visited them from time to time. Aikelos kept my special paste under the counter – told her it was a very rare thing, only for the very best and most daring cooks. I knew she was famous amongst the selkies for her cooking, but had lost her Gold Cup to another cook recently, so Aikelos played on her pride. And so she fell in with my plans, without even realising it...' She laid her cool hand again on Thomas's one, and he felt that odd shiver rippling over him from head to foot. But he couldn't drag his eyes away from Cirsea's face now. In the fog of his brain, only one thing kept repeating, over and over: She's so lovely . . . so good . . . so kind . . .

'You've seen for yourself, Thomas, how they're not as sick as they should be. The curse has been pushed back, a little. But it's not enough. It must be undone completely, dissolve, melt . . . And only you can do that.'

'Only me? But you will help me, won't you?' said Thomas, anxiously. 'You're so kind and good . . . so kind and good . . . Oh, I'm so sorry that the selkies are mean and unjust to you . . . I will make sure they know everything and—'

'Not yet, my sweet,' said Cirsea, flashing a glance at her servant as she spoke. 'You must go first and find the one thing that will undo the curse – and though I cannot come with you on this journey, Aikelos will. He has a very swift boat and will take you up this very night. You will bring it back here, and then together we will undo the curse – just as that first Rymer and my dear ancestress did, long, long ago . . .' She paused, and smiled sweetly up at Thomas. 'Are you ready, dear, dear Thomas? Are you ready to brave the dangers that first Rymer faced, and bring back the one thing that can undo the curse?'

'Oh yes,' said Thomas, dreamily. 'Oh yes, I am ready. What is it you want me to bring? What will undo the curse?'

'Why, Maldict, of course,' said the Syren,

quietly. 'Maldict, the Book of Curses – the most remarkable book in all of the worlds.'

'Oh,' said Thomas, giving a little shiver. A picture flashed through the fog in his mind, of a thing baggy and pale as a sea snake, rising from a basket. He went on, slowly, 'I know Maldict. I have seen it. Oh! And I think I heard your voice, then, too.'

'The Kin had something to do with the compiling of that book,' said Cirsea, her eyes searching his face. 'It carries the echo of our voices. Now then, Thomas, there is no time to be lost. Maldict must be fetched, and fetched at once.'

Thomas stammered, 'You want *me* to get Maldict? But . . .'

For the first time, the Syren frowned. 'Are you afraid, Thomas?'

'No . . . no,' faltered Thomas, 'but . . . but you said the antidote you made is working, and so I—'

'It won't work for ever,' snapped Cirsea. 'In

fact, it may well stop working quite soon. And if it does, then the curse will rage unchecked and many selkies will die.' Her voice dropped. 'And it's quite likely that your friend Roanna will be one of those who die . . . The curse killed many young selkies, that first time.'

The selkie girl's name pierced Thomas's misted mind like an arrow. He said, quietly, 'You sent her the message that was supposed to be from me, didn't you?'

'Of course,' said the Syren, softly. 'You see, she had talked a lot about her encounter with the Rymer – that's another thing selkies do, talk a lot . . . It was the one sure way of making you come.'

'But the map,' said Thomas, slowly, 'the map you sent her – it was wrong. She nearly died.'

'She risked her life to find you,' said Cirsea, 'but she is no map-reader, Thomas, dear.'

'The map was wrong,' Thomas repeated, stubbornly. 'It was wrong.'

The Syren's eyes glittered with temper. 'Are

you ready to do what must be done, or are you afraid and trying to find a way out? Are you ready to accept then that because of you, many, many selkies will die? Don't you care about your friend Roanna? I was told friendship meant a good deal to humans. Now I see I was wrong. You care more about your own skin.'

The mist was still fogging up Thomas's mind, but he could see a little more clearly now, in brief snatches. He faltered, 'I didn't say I wouldn't do it. If it's the only thing that will save the selkies, I will do it. But I don't understand how Maldict can—'

'You do not need to understand,' snapped Cirsea. 'Not yet, anyway,' she added, more gently, as Thomas stared at her, wide-eyed. 'My sweet, my pretty,' she crooned, laying her hand on his own, 'my dearest Rymer . . .'

As she crooned, Thomas could feel the tendrils of enchanted mist filling his head again. But he struggled against it this time. He must not give in to it. He must not. He suddenly remembered, as if in a dream, Old Gal offering him earplugs. He'd left them by his bed . . . But maybe there was some way . . . some other way of shutting out that voice . . .

'I'll do it,' he faltered. 'I will fetch Maldict for you.' My friends, he thought. I must think of them. Not only Roanna, but Pinch and Patch. Old Gal. Calliope. Pandora. As he thought the names, the mist began to clear again. He repeated them to himself. Cirsea's voice kept crooning on, but he saw his friends' names, bright and clear in the fog, which was fading, fading . . . He thought, I must not let her see. I must let her think I'm still quite in her power, I must act as if I'm all in a fog. And I must repeat my friends' names to myself, over and over and over . . . Pinch and Patch, and Roanna, and Delfinus, and Old Gal, and Calliope and Pandora . . . more names came to him . . . and Angelica, and Adverse, and Dad . . . oh Dad, and Mum, who's not there any more but who I think watches over me still . . . I'm Thomas, Thomas Trew, and these are my friends, and my family . . .

'Sweet Thomas, dear Thomas,' said the Syren, and this time, when she smiled, Thomas saw her sharp white teeth. 'You are a brave boy, a brave Rymer. Now, to fetch Maldict out, do you know what you must do?'

'It likes music,' said Thomas, slowly, speaking as if with an effort, making his eyes vague. 'I heard the bookseller playing a tune, a strange, spooky tune . . .'

'That's right,' said the Syren. 'Aikelos! You are to take Thomas back at once to the surface, and to his village. You are to take my bone flute with you.' She looked at Thomas. 'It will play a very similar tune. When you are close to the book, put the flute to your mouth. It will play of its own accord. Play it, and the book will follow you back here. Then we can undo the curse. Do you understand, my sweet?'

'Yes, I understand,' said Thomas, drowsily,

playing at being spellbound while he kept his mind busy, repeating his friends' names. 'But why, my lady, couldn't you have come to Owlchurch and played the bone flute yourself and made Maldict follow you?'

'I should have liked to, very much, but the Kin are forbidden to go into Middler lands,' said Cirsea, harshly. 'Everyone is unjust to us, everyone. Besides, I am purely a saltwater being, and cannot survive even an instant in sweet water. If I set even a scale in sweet water, then I will die. And I cannot travel by air, for Ariel lands are closed to me too, and those of the Montaynards . . . and even underground I dare not . . .' She trailed off, looking sad.

'Oh,' said Thomas, 'that is a very great pity . . .' But inside he was very glad. That meant the Syren couldn't do much once he was away from the sea. Unfortunately, though, Aikelos must be able to survive sweet water to some extent or it would not be able to escort him to Owlchurch . . . He'd have to try and lose it as soon as possible.

'You are a good boy. A brave Rymer,' said Cirsea, sweetly. 'And don't be sad for me, dear Thomas. Things will change, once I have Maldict. There is a certain powerful lord who has spurned my advances but will change his tune when—' She saw Thomas's expression and hurried on, 'But that is for later. For now, dear Rymer, fetch me Maldict, that we may undo this dastardly curse and your friends be freed . . .'

'And your name will be praised throughout the Hidden World,' said Thomas, eagerly. 'It will be praised and renowned . . .'

'Oh, that it will be,' said Cirsea, smiling rather horribly. 'That it will be, dear boy.' She waved a hand at Aikelos. 'Off you go. There is no time to be lost. And remember, Aikelos – you are not to lay a hand on the Rymer, or you'll have to answer to me for it. Is that clear?'

'Yes, my lady,' said Aikelos, cringing, though

his little eyes glowed red with anger and disappointment.

The Syren glanced at Thomas, who was looking vaguely into the distance, trying to look spellbound. Under her breath, she murmured to her servant, 'Of course, once we have the book here, things will be rather different . . .'

'Very well, my lady,' said Aikelos, brightening. 'Come on, dear Rymer, dear master,' it said in its sly, falsely humble voice. 'Come with me, dear sweet young master Rymer.'

NINETEEN

Pinch and Patch woke in the early morning and found Thomas gone. 'His bed's cold,' said Patch. 'Pinch, I don't think he's been here for hours . . .'

'He took the sea-light,' said Pinch, blankly. 'So he must have gone out when it was still dark.'

The twins looked at each other. 'I think we'd better go and look for him,' said Patch.

They flung on their clothes and slipped out of the room. The house was quiet. Everyone still seemed to be asleep. They tiptoed down the two sets of stairs to the ground floor. Passing the banquet-hall, they could hear faint noises. They poked their noses around the door.

Roanna and Telegon were in there, helping themselves to dishes on the sideboard. They jumped rather guiltily when Pinch spoke.

'Hey! Seen Thomas?'

Roanna stared. 'No. Why?'

'He's gone,' said Patch, 'and we don't know where he is. I think he's gone off investigating on his own,' she added, disapprovingly.

The selkies looked at each other. 'Investigating what?' said Telegon.

'Your silly curse,' snapped Patch.

'It's not silly,' Roanna began, 'it's—'

'Oh, never mind,' said Pinch, crossly. 'Thing is, he thought there was something fishy going on . . .'

'Eh?' said Telegon. 'What do fish have to do with it? They're not part of the curse, you know.'

Pinch rolled his eyes. 'Never mind.' He turned to Patch. 'They don't know anything. Let's go and look for—'

'We'll come with you,' said Roanna. 'We

know this place better than you do,' she added, firmly, as the twins looked likely to argue.

'Well, OK. Everything's quiet upstairs,' said Patch, resignedly.

'They're all asleep. They had a big night,' said Telegon. 'That's why we thought we'd come down early and get the best of the smoked herring before it all goes . . .' He cast a longing look at the sideboard. 'I think we shouldn't do anything on an empty stomach, do you?'

'Well . . .' Pinch began.

Patch quelled him with a fierce glare. 'We'll have breakfast when we find Thomas,' she said. 'Anyway, Pinch, you know you don't like smoked herring.'

'No,' grumbled Pinch, 'but that doesn't mean I—'

'I agree,' said Roanna, surprisingly. 'I think we should find Thomas first. It probably won't take long.'

'He might have gone looking for something

179

to eat in the kitchen,' suggested Telegon, looking sadly at the herring. 'He might have been hungry . . .'

'Oh, Tel!' sighed Roanna. 'One-track mind, you have.'

But Patch said, 'Maybe you're right. He hardly ate anything at dinner-time, did you notice, Pinch? On second thoughts, you were too busy filling your face . . . Maybe he just woke up and felt really hungry . . . maybe he just went down to look for some food.'

'But he took the sea-light,' said Pinch. 'That must mean it was dark. If he went down to find something to eat, then he's been gone a while.'

'He might have fallen asleep,' said Telegon, eagerly. 'I do sometimes if I've had a big meal.'

But he spoke to empty air. The others had already gone. Snatching up a herring and cramming it whole into his mouth, Telegon followed them.

'I can smell something,' said Roanna, wrinkling

her nose, as they hurried down the twisty stairs.

'Something fishy,' snickered Pinch.

'No, no, not a nice clean fishy smell. Something dark and ugly. Tel – do you smell it too?'

'Yes,' said Telegon, rather uncertainly. 'Roanna, I think it smells like . . .'

'Like what?' snapped Patch.

'Like fin-folk,' said Roanna. 'Oh, you won't know them,' she added. 'They are—'

'Oh, we know what they are,' butted in Pinch. 'Like Peg and Nelly and them. Water-prowlers. Scavengers. Sly hunters. Nasty individuals with shark fins on their backs.'

'I didn't know selkies employed fin-folk,' said Patch.

'Are you crazy?' said Roanna. 'Of course we don't. They're dirty, sly and treacherous. They usually work on their own account, though a few of them work for Syrens.'

'Well, then, what's a fin-folk person doing here?' said Patch.

'I don't know,' said Roanna. 'And I don't like it.'

'I don't either,' said Telegon, eagerly.

'Oh good, good, I feel so relieved about that,' murmured Pinch, sarcastically, as they hurried down the last few stairs.

There were already servants busily working in the kitchen, rolling out pastry and baking bread. They didn't seem to think it strange to see the children come in – Roanna and Telegon were obviously frequent visitors to the kitchens. They seemed to be in a fluster, but it was nothing to do with Thomas, whom they hadn't seen at all. It was to do with the fact that Miss Clytie, the head cook, must have overslept for she hadn't come down to the kitchen yet, and there were all the day's menus to go through, and a new batch of Proteus Puddings to make . . .

'They're all scared of her,' whispered Roanna to the others.

'She's a bit of a caution, she is,' agreed

Telegon. 'Bet no one wants to go up there and wake her!'

The servants also said that though they had noticed a funny smell, they had opened the windows and it had gone away. And did the children want to leave them in peace to work now? How about a nice fresh roll in payment? No one refused that!

While they were busy munching, the children also took a good look around. But there was no sign of Thomas anywhere. Roanna said she thought the flour sacks in the pantry had been moved, but that didn't mean anything. They went out none the wiser, and stood around in the passageway outside, trying to decide what to do next.

'I think that the fin-folk have something to do with this,' said Patch, thoughtfully. 'Maybe – do you think they've kidnapped Thomas?'

There was a small silence. 'Don't be silly,' said Pinch, uneasily. 'Why should they?'

'Well, maybe they just wanted to get

Thomas here so they could snatch him. I mean, *someone* must have written that message, pretending to be from the Rymer.'

Roanna laughed. 'Oh, not the fin-folk. They can't read or write. And they're not that bright, either.'

'Well, it's still strange they've been here on the very night Thomas vanishes,' said Patch, stubbornly.

'We don't know he's vanished,' said Pinch, reasonably.

His sister glared at him. 'Well, where is he then?'

'I don't know. Taking a walk . . .'

'Out there, in the dark?'

'Wait a moment . . .' Roanna's bright eyes had caught sight of something flashing in the corner. She darted over to it. 'Oh – it's just a piece of glass . . . Someone must have dropped a glass and not swept it up properly . . .'

'That's not from a glass,' said Telegon. 'Give it here, Ro.' He looked at the shard of glass.

'That's thicker and has different properties – from a lamp, I'd say.' He looked at the others, flushing a little. 'I'm kind of interested in glass-blowing. You see, you need different kinds from every—'

'A lamp?' broke in Pinch. 'Thomas took the sea-light with him . . .'

They looked at each other.

'Someone broke a lamp – someone swept all the bits away, except they missed that one – there's a smell of the fin-folk around . . .' said Roanna, slowly.

Telegon was walking back and forth, sniffing carefully. 'I think it went this way,' he said, pointing. 'Down to the cellar.'

'But the gate's got to be unlocked,' said Roanna, as they all hurried off. 'It can't have got in or out without someone here helping it . . .'

Telegon looked grim. 'I don't like it,' he said. 'I don't like it at all.'

'Who does?' snapped Pinch, exasperated.

There was no one in the cellar, of course. But the selkies said it still smelled strongly of fin-folk. Sniffing carefully at the gate, they also said, rather doubtfully, that they thought it smelled a bit of human too, as if someone had squeezed out through there. Pinch and Patch looked at the heavy gate and thought of the big sea outside and Thomas maybe out there, and the stories they had heard of fin-folk and their man-eating ways, and began to feel a little sick. And very scared.

'Even if he's just gone out to investigate,' said Patch, slowly, 'he's only had one dose of Mother's protective potion. If they catch him, even if they don't . . . they don't hurt him, he won't last long without the potion. He'll start to drown . . .' She gulped. 'I think we've got to go and get help straight away from the adults. We can't do this on our own. They've got to send out a search party, at once.'

Pinch was about to argue, but a look at his sister's face changed his mind. He didn't want to admit it of course but he was more scared than he had been in a long time. The sea was not his element either.

Roanna said, eagerly, 'We don't need to involve any adults yet. It's maybe hard for you, but Tel and I can go out there no problem . . . we can try and follow his trail . . .'

'No!' shouted Patch. 'You've caused enough trouble, you have! You made us come here, to the horrid old sea! It's your fault if something bad happens to Thomas!'

'Patch, that's not fair . . .' Pinch began, uneasily. But Patch had turned on her heel and ran away from them, up the cellar steps, down the passage and back up the stairs, sobbing as she went.

Pinch looked at the others. He winced. 'Sorry,' he said, awkwardly. 'She didn't mean it. It's just she's so worried . . .'

'I know,' said Roanna, gently. She bent her head. 'And she's right, you know . . . it *is* my fault. I should have let well alone.

Grandmother and the others would have sorted it out in time.'

'I doubt it,' said Pinch, firmly. 'Given as how Maldict said a Rymer solved it last time. Come on, Roanna, don't you go all mushy. It won't help us find Thomas. Besides, you were very brave to come to us.'

'You really mean that?' said Roanna, quietly.

Pinch nodded. 'I do.' After a little pause, he went on, 'And I think Patch is right – I mean, about getting help,' he hurried on.

'I think so too,' said Telegon, eagerly. 'I think we should, Ro. I really do. I don't mind telling you I really don't like any of this . . . not at all . . .'

Roanna and Pinch looked at each other and burst out laughing. Telegon looked mystified, but then good-naturedly joined in the laughter, too.

TWENTY

Meanwhile, Thomas was far away above them, speeding over the sea in Aikelos's shark-shaped boat, and trying to think of a way to send a warning message to Owlchurch. If only he'd had a chance to snatch up a few dream-boats! But he hadn't, and that was that.

Since they'd left, he'd been trying to look as though he was still enchanted – mouth open, eyes staring glassily. He could breathe much more easily up in the air too of course, so it made his brain feel a lot sharper. He had remembered now about the fin-folk. He could see Aikelos's file-sharp teeth flash in its lipless mouth, and he knew that if it hadn't been for the fact the creature was terrified of the Syren, it might have pounced on him. As it was, he should be safe enough – that is, until he brought Maldict back.

But of course he wasn't going to do that at all. Once he was back in Owlchurch, he was going to tell Monotype to lock the book away somewhere very safe, hold it down with the strongest spells possible, and capture Aikelos. But he felt uneasy. He had the Syren's bone flute in his pocket. Would it stay quiet? It was a nasty thing, made of bleached bone, with a silver mouthpiece, and carved all over with snakes and skulls. The Syren had told him it wasn't a human bone, but rather that of some sea snake creature that had been the pet of some long-ago Syren. Thomas hoped that was true. It was certainly much thinner than a human bone. But you certainly couldn't trust what the Syren said. She'd told a lot of lies, though with the truth underneath, hiding like a snake in the grass.

She must have called the curse herself, he thought. But how? Roanna had definitely said it could only be called by selkies. But somehow Cirsea must have found a way. And maybe that was why the curse was weaker than it should be, because it wasn't a selkie who had called it. She must have planned the whole thing all along, he thought. She must have pinched that tune from the Lochlans, made them think it was the Proteans, and then one of her spies had overheard the furious Lochlans threatening to curse them, and hey presto, she called the curse!

Thomas looked over at Aikelos. The fin-man seemed to be asleep, his hood drawn over his face. Thomas watched the sea and thought carefully. Cirsea must have called the curse not because she hated the selkies but because she wanted to get hold of Maldict. It must be the only way she could do it, if she was forbidden to travel outside of the sea. She had to target a human being, not a Hidden Worlder, who is immune to her enchantments. And as a Rymer was mentioned as having broken the curse in Maldict, that was so much the better. She had no interest in Thomas himself, only in him getting the book for her.

As to *why* she wanted it . . . For power, of course. For herself, and also – yes, she'd mentioned some lord or other who had 'spurned her advances'. That meant that he'd rejected her. Maybe she wanted to marry him, whoever he was, and he'd refused? She hadn't said who it was, but that he'd 'change his tune' when she got Maldict. That meant the lord, whoever it was, wanted to get hold of Maldict too.

'Oh, gosh!' The startled exclamation burst out before he could control it. Aikelos woke up. It glared redly at Thomas. But its voice was soft as it said, 'What's the matter, Rymer?'

'Oh, nothing . . .' said Thomas, vaguely. 'I thought I saw a flying fish.' He grinned stupidly. 'It had wings like a little plane . . . I thought it was going to swoop me and try and stop me from my great task . . .'

'You're barmy, Rymer,' said Aikelos, glaring at him. 'Anyone would think you're happy to be going on this trip.'

'Oh, but I'm going to undo the curse! I'm going to help the Lady Cirsea! Oh, Aikelos, isn't she the dearest, sweetest, most wonderful lady who ever lived!'

Thomas thought he might have overdone the enthusiasm, but Aikelos apparently didn't think so. It smiled horribly. 'You poor fool,' it murmured, and its ugly grey tongue darted over its lipless mouth. 'You poor fool, you don't even have an inkling what's in store for you,' it murmured.

'Oh, Aikelos,' said Thomas, brightly, 'your mistress is so clever, so wonderful! And yet those silly selkies hate her . . . it seems so unfair. But she must know so much about them, so much.'

'Oh, a good deal, a good deal,' said Aikelos,

grinning toothily. 'A good deal about everything . . . For instance, she knows that sweetwater sickness can unbalance their fine-tuning. She also knows pearls come in two varieties.' He glanced sideways at Thomas. 'Do you understand what I'm saying, Rymer?'

Thomas tried to keep the excitement from showing on his face. He beamed foolishly and said, 'No, I do not, but what I am sure your mistress does. She must know everything in the world!'

'Oh, she knows most things,' the fin-man smirked, 'and most especially how to deal with humans like you. Though why she should think you're any good as a Rymer, I don't know,' it muttered. 'You seem pretty daft to me.'

'I imagine there must be many great lords wanting to marry her,' said Thomas, still beaming, as if he hadn't heard those last words.

The fin-man looked sharply at him. 'There is at that,' he muttered. 'But the one that she wants – he's not biting. Not yet. But he will. He will, when he sees the gift she brings with her! He's wanted it for so long, Rymer, so long . . . and together, he and my mistress will make a couple who will have all the worlds at their feet, and rule in power and glory for ever!'

Thomas said nothing, just looked wondering and amazed. But inside he was thinking, now I know! Now I know *how* she did it, and *why*!

The search party for Thomas had been out for quite a while before anyone thought of looking for Clytie. When they did find her in a tavern near the city gates, she was already too far gone in seaweed wine to question properly. But she babbled about a fin-man named Aikelos, and a certain pearl-paste, bought illegally from a midnight stall, and Proteus Pudding, and a lamp, dropped in the passage, and the smell of a human behind a cellar door . . . and how her career was ruined . . . and oh, she'd destroyed that last batch he'd brought her, because she thought there was something very wrong, and oh . . . she'd go to prison happily if only she could wind it all back . . . back . . .

Back at the Protean mansion, Old Gal had fired off two urgent dream-boats, telling Angelica and Mr Tamblin what had happened, and asking them to send a rescue party of their own immediately. She went off to get Calliope and Pandora, for as she said, her own powers were not enough to find Thomas in the maze of dark alleyways where the fin-man might have taken him. Nobody knew yet that Aikelos was a servant of Cirsea's . . . but it wouldn't be long . . .

And there now at last was the mouth of the river. Aikelos turned the shark-boat sharply left and raced through the water, whizzing past forest and field at an unlikely speed. Thomas began to feel very dizzy; but looking at Aikelos, he could see that the fin-man did

not look very comfortable himself. He thought, I wonder, I wonder . . .

They flashed past a bend in the river, then another. The long silver ribbon of the Riddle glittered. And then, with a roar, and a jerk, the boat drew up at the deserted Owlchurch landing-stage. Thomas was flung backwards, and fell on to the deck, winded. Then Aikelos was looming over him, shouting and waving a fist. 'Hurry! Hurry! Something's wrong! They've rumbled us! They've put a spell on me! I feel sick! The flute, fool! The flute!'

The fin-man looked ghastly. Or rather, more ghastly than ever. Its grey face had become tinged with a horrible shade of green, its eyes spun wildly in their sockets, it was trembling and shaking like a leaf. 'Get out the flute,' screamed the creature, 'or Lady Cirsea or not, I'll bite you in two!' Its wicked teeth clattered close to Thomas's ear.

Trembling, Thomas put his hand in his pocket and drew out the flute. It wriggled in his hand, and then, horrifyingly, leaped up to his mouth and clung there like a limpet, or a leech. Thomas cried out and tried to strike the flute away, but it wouldn't let go of him.

Aikelos was screaming, laughing like a mad thing. 'Play, flute, play! Play for my lady!'

Thomas could see people coming now, running down the hill towards the river. He could see his father, and Adverse, and Cumulus, and Morph, and Hinkypunk, and Monotype . . .

'No, no!' he wanted to shout. 'Stay with the book!'

But Monotype couldn't hear him, and anyway the flute was stopping his words, choking him, covering his mouth. He tried to pull it off, and thought he was about to manage, but Aikelos landed on top of him and forced it back to his lips. It screamed, 'Play, flute, play, damn you! Play for my lady, and her dowry! Play! Play! For all the worlds we will gain and the power and the destruction . . .'

'No,' Thomas tried to say, 'never,' but the flute took his words and turned them into a long, drawn-out note, a terrible, strange, spooky note that made the hair rise on end and limbs seem to turn to stone. Thomas was helpless as the bone flute kept playing, and playing, and it was like in a dream – the people running down towards him never seemed to get any closer, and he couldn't move from the flute fastened on his lips and he couldn't stop playing it. Then he heard the Syren's voice in his head, crooning, crooning, 'Come to me, my sweet, my pretty . . . come, Maldict, come to me . . . and we will go home, you and I, we will go to your lord who will be mine too . . . Come, my sweet, come, my honey, come, my darling one . . .'

And in his mind's eye, Thomas saw, clear as clear, a vision of Maldict bursting out from its basket, its blind head questing, its shapeless form oozing out into the shop, flowing silently and baggily out into the street, and down the hill towards the river . . . The flute played again, and the Syren's voice called, this time outside Thomas's head, ringing clear as a bell over Owlchurch: 'Come, come, my pretty – for our time has come!'

'Yes, yes!' screamed Aikelos. 'Come, Maldict – and we will bring the Rymer, dead or alive, too, to offer to your gracious lord!'

'Oh, no you don't!' said a voice, quite close to Thomas's ear, and then there was a splash, and a terrible shriek as Aikelos hit the water, turned black, swelled, then burst like a smelly balloon. In the next instant, even those fragments were gone. 'Oh, no you don't, whoever you are!' said the voice again. A hand reached over and pulled the flute from Thomas's lips and flung it overboard, where it vanished with a steaming hiss. Then Thomas was picked up bodily and his rescuer jumped off the boat with him, landing with a thump. 'Oh, no you don't!' said Thomas's father, angrier than Thomas had ever seen him, trying to hold back his son from struggling free.

'But, Dad, you don't understand! I have to go! I have to stop Maldict!' said Thomas, wriggling as hard as he could.

'Somebody else can do that,' said Gareth, sternly. 'You've done quite enough . . . Quite enough,' he repeated, more furiously than ever. 'I won't have it, do you hear? I won't have it!'

And to his astonishment, Thomas looked up and saw that his father's eyes were swimming with tears and that his Adam's apple was bobbing up and down. He felt his father's arms tighten around him, and heard him say, 'Oh, Thomas . . . I thought I'd lost you . . . I thought I'd lost you, for ever . . . I couldn't bear that, Thomas, I couldn't, I couldn't . . .'

Thomas hugged his father tightly, and said, rather awkwardly, 'It's all right, Dad, I'm all right, really I am. Really. Oh, Dad, you were great, just then! Oh, Dad, I've got so much to tell you!'

'And there's quite a few of us want to hear it, Thomas Trew,' said Angelica's voice, behind them. She looked grim and relieved, all at once. 'Thank goodness you're safe. Those selkies – I think it's time they learned to solve their own problems.'

'They're not under a curse,' said Thomas, excitedly. 'It was just a kind of poison – something that was being fed to them,

202

something they liked but that made them ill . . .'

'Yes,' said Angelica. 'It was in that Proteus Pudding they were so fond of, wasn't it? Its main ingredient was a pearl-paste – but made not of sea-pearls but freshwater pearls. Oysters live in both sorts of water, you see. Well, it affected their fine-tuning, their ear for music, but it was no curse, it just looked like it was.'

'How do you know all that?' said Thomas, staring, and Angelica waved a hand up to the sky. Thomas saw a dot up there, a white dot that came closer and closer, and soon resolved itself into the Aspire limousine! As it came closer, lower, he could see a whole lot of people squashed in there, waving. There were Pinch and Patch, their faces right up to the glass – and yes, the selkie cousins, too!

'Your friends went looking for you,' said Angelica, gently. 'All of them – the twins, and Roanna, and Telegon. You have a talent for making friends, Thomas. And for binding friends together – for they all seem to have

quite a liking for each other now, I'm told. That's a great gift.'

By this time, the other Owlchurchers had come running up, the bookseller ahead of the others. 'My dear boy, my dear boy,' he kept repeating, 'if I'd known it was that wicked old Maldict they were after, I can tell you, I'd not have let it out of its basket, not once!'

'You couldn't help it. After all, it did say that the first Rymer had undone the curse. And so Thomas has, too,' said Angelica, gently.

'In a way, I suppose I did,' said Thomas, thoughtfully. 'But not in the way he did. The Syren told me a pack of lies about it all, but I suppose that part of it was true.'

'Oh, it was,' said Monotype. 'He had quite a gift for medicine, you see. He actually made up an antidote for them – nothing to do with pearls or puddings – and dosed the selkies with it. That's what gave the Syren the idea for her plot.'

'Oh, I see. Maldict didn't get away, did it?'

said Thomas, anxiously.

'Oh, no, no, it tried to, but I gave it a good solid thump on the head,' said Adverse Camber, grimly. 'It'll see stars for a good while to come. I vote we weight it down with chains and drown it . . .'

'Oh no,' said Monotype, earnestly. 'No, no, not after what happened. We have to keep it here, but well-hidden, and never let it out. For any reason.'

'Besides,' said Thomas, 'if we drown it, the Syren might find it one day, and take it to General Legion Morningstar, in the Uncouthers' country.' They all stared at him. 'You see, I think she wanted to marry him,' he said, smiling a little at their astonishment. 'I think she wanted to bring him Maldict as a wedding gift. She thought that together they could make plans to rule over all the worlds . . .'

He stopped as the limousine landed a short distance away. The doors opened, and the twins tumbled out. They came running towards Thomas, Pinch shouting, 'Guess what happened! Guess what happened! The selkies have made peace! And the Duchess has arrested that Syren!'

'She's going to prison for a long, long time, for poisoning the selkies and kidnapping you and trying to make a deal with Uncouthers!' gasped Patch, excitedly.

Behind the twins, unusually shy, came Roanna and Telegon. As they drew near, Roanna murmured, 'Did you know – it was in that Proteus Pudding, Thomas – that was what was making us sick . . . Poor Clytie. She feels so bad.'

'Well, she was tricked. And after all, everyone liked the pudding,' said Thomas.

'Everyone except me,' said Telegon, proudly. 'And I really, *really* didn't like it,' he added, amid their gales of laughter, 'no sir, not one little, tiny bit!'

THOMAS TREW AND THE HIDDEN PEOPLE

Sophie Masson

Thomas feels different from other people.
He sees things no one else sees.
He hears things no one else hears.
It feels as if he's waiting for something to happen.

Then one day it does.
A truly extraordinary person appears in his home.

A dwarf.

And this is only the beginning of his
extraordinary journey . . .

THOMAS TREW AND THE HORNS OF PAN

Sophie Masson

Thomas loves living in the Hidden World.
His friends, the twins Pinch and Patch,
are even teaching him magic, like how to
make himself invisible.

Then a beautiful stranger comes to Owlchurch.
She holds the Horns of Pan, the Hidden World's
highest award for magic.

Everyone is excited – except Thomas and the twins.
Something very odd is going on,
and they're determined to find out . . .

THOMAS TREW AND THE KLINT-KING'S GOLD

Sophie Masson

Thomas is fascinated by the great Magicians' and
Enchanters' Convention in Owlchurch – hundreds of
human witches, magicians, enchanters and wizards
competing in magic tournaments against each other
and the Hidden People.

The king of the mountainous Klint Kingdom,
Reidmar Redbard, is even offering marvellous gold
prizes, dripping with jewels.

But there's more than just fun and enjoyment going
on. Thomas and his friends are soon on the trail of a
hidden and very dangerous enemy.

h HODDER *Read more Thomas Trew adventures . . .*

Coming soon . . .

THOMAS TREW AND THE FLYING HUNTSMAN

Sophie Masson

The breathtaking land of the Ariels floats in the clouds, rich in powerful magic.

But hidden dangers hover there. With his ravening pack of dogs, the wild and terrifying Flying Huntsman stalks the skies astride his brutish horse.

On a visit to Ariel country, Thomas is snatched from his friends. Is the Flying Huntsman behind his disappearance, or is another enemy on the loose?

Read more Thomas Trew adventures . . .

Coming soon . . .

THOMAS TREW AND THE ISLAND OF GHOSTS

Sophie Masson

A mysterious island appears in the River Riddle.
The Island of Ghosts – dark and dangerous, where
ghosts of past Rymers dwell in afterlife. It can mean
only one thing: a living Rymer is in mortal danger.
There's only one known Rymer alive. Thomas Trew.

Thomas can't bear to leave his friends for the
safety of London. He has his own daring plan
to search the island and seek help from the ghost
of his mother. And so awaits a dark and
dangerous adventure for Thomas . . .